Runaway with the Wind

The Diary of a Small Person

Dan Brady

ISBN 13: 978-0692134979
ISBN 10: 0692134972

First Edition, 2017
Second Edition, 2026

One Insight Press
San Francisco, Ca

Please see my author's page
https://www.amazon.com/Dan-Brady/e/
B014ROHMNC

Acknowledgements:

I don't now know where the idea for this story came from. The original hand written drafts were composed in the early to mid 1970's, seemingly eons ago. I wrote the original manuscript in pencil partly during lunch breaks at work or slow moments between dispatch calls. The diary format suited those circumstances. So, while it may have come from a dream, a conversation, or even an idle comment, its source remains a mystery. I did set Jan's meandering journey in the San Francisco Bay Area, using maps, and news stories, current at the time, as well as childhood memories for verity's sake.

One of the characters, Mr. Fish, is modeled after someone my mom knew. They worked at Agnew's State Hospital for several years and he visited our home a few times. I cannot recollect which tribe he belonged to but he was taciturn, soft-spoken, big, easy-going, and told stories. The one I recollect best happened during World War Two, in the Philippines. He had become isolated behind enemy lines and was starving. At night, during a heavy downpour, he killed a Japanese soldier, who was about his size and quickly changed into the man's uniform. Later, he got in step with other Japanese soldiers, and then, went into their camp, through its chow line, and was well fed by his enemies.

In general, the contour of the story, as well as some of its elements, reflect the kind of Sci-Fi I read growing up – not to mention certain television shows.

Dan

Introduction:

This is a dairy of a small person, Jan. I purposely did not specify Jan's gender. Originally, because of the way the inspiration arrived, I felt I couldn't decide what to do with this essential aspect of the character– nor did this matter clarify as I wrote. I "split the difference" and kept true to the vague nature of my original notion. I thought, in a practical way, this choice might widen the appeal by making it more inclusive. Some of what happens to Jan at the beginning of the story came from tales told to me by childhood friends or things in the local news way back when.

Jan's special talents are based on some of my own personal experiences, those of friends, and or from the inspirational moments which came to transpire during the course of my writing this story.

Table of Contents

********************** **********************
# Jan's Cover Letter
********************** **********************

Dear Mom,

I wanted very much for you to have this but getting it back to you wasn't at all easy. My friend thought it would be too dangerous for me. At that time I was younger and so he was the one who went. At first, he didn't dare go anywhere near your place, directly, for fear of being recognized. Even though he wasn't sure if you were still living at the old place or what had happened - it was all he knew to do. He could tell the place was being watched so, by hook and crook, he did see to it that this was put into the mail slot. However, he had to be pretty damned tricky in order to get away clean, even then, in one instance, he had to fight his way clear at knifepoint.

I was very glad that, at least for a while, you and Vince were doing better. However, I enjoy living "up here." I love what I'm doing. So, although I can come back, if you're reading this it's proof that it can be done, my intention is to stay. In part because of how my friend was treated, which indicates how I'll be treated, and in part because when I looked at the papers my friend brought back they showed plenty of reasons for not coming back to your world.

I know you never looked in my diary except that once very early on – but I want you to read it now. In it you'll find out about my friends, the one who brought the diary back, Joey, and Wind. None of them think anything is wrong with sending this to you.

When we got to this place, and were safe enough to rest, I stopped writing pretty much but after a while, I decided to rewrite it because it was jumbled up. When it was done I talked my friend into getting it back to you.

Although I don't know whether or not to believe him, my friend says I'll be going back but I can't promise something I don't feel is true. Maybe I need a chance for peace. I need to figure out what I should do when I do return and how to deal with the problems my talent attracts.

He and I wrote a song, in his language, it talks about some of the things I'm thinking about.

A gift of mountains

Saying that you talk to mountains
by listening
only to the light that flows through both of you
is
the quietest way
to understand
that reach of breath;
to know,
to have it-
to stretch out my arms to the stars
to my dreams
to the night
to touch
the smallest idea
the largest star!
I want to know my pasts
future
and the balance of me
in this time
in this aura
of presence.
I create the mountains
resting in their age
for ages
I've been here
writing this
for you
alone.

Once you read this you'll see that you do not have to have people looking for me or try to catch me. I'm fine; I even went to the dentist for a filling, on my own, how about that? I don't like lying, you know that, though I've had to lie when I lived the way I did back there – I've learned to do many things I don't like simply to survive. I love you mom. I've got to find out what it is I want to do with my talents.

Mom, there's one more thing.

The strangest thing is I don't dream much way up here. But in the few dreams I do have I'm now either Joey or he is I, I can't always tell which. I mostly don't go out in my dreams there is nothing much in this world except nature, animals, the land, and ocean. I still search the stars for other worlds. There are plenty of them, some with simple life on them, but nothing like what's on Earth. Around where I am there are no other people except for the ones riding along inside their own magic boulders. My friend says he thinks there must be some others like us here. He has heard that some do open up every once in a great while though I'll believe it when I see it.
One more thing I miss you. I promise. I'll find a way to make it better for you and everyone, Jan.

*********************** *********************

The Diary's Introduction

*********************** *********************

3/18/83

I am making a diary. I had to wait a long time to do this; I mean to say it seemed like eons and manaventeras. Mrs. Ernst at school says I am way beyond my years. She says I can write very well, indeed. I like that word, indeed I do. This makes me laugh almost out loud. On the way home today I felt I could run like the wind. I was so happy. I had made up my mind to buy this book, this one right here. Last summer Tim told me about the kind of book with blank pages inside and ever since then I wanted one.

I had to save from my lunch or milk money for weeks and weeks. Vince said he would get me one of them for my birthday although when my birthday came I did not get the book, of course, and, of course, he said he'd forgotten. I was disappointed mostly like always. He got mad when I asked about it. He gets mad easily. I am learning to map out the things that get him angry so I can avoid doing any of them. Tim said I could write anything in the diary; that's what they are for. He said you have to give your diary a name. I do not have a name for mine yet.

My name is Jan. My mom's name is Marie Bellum-Real while my horrid stepfather's name is Vincent Real; he tells everyone to call him Vinie. He likes it that way. I live in Alamo, California in the United States, on the world, which goes around the sun, Sol. I am 10 years old. I like to read. My real dad is dead. He died in a car accident when I was only almost six. We lived in a real big city, way back east, New York City. My mom told me a drunken driver hit my dad as he was getting into his car. She took me back to California. She always said she wanted to come back here to live. She was born in Sacramento but when she left her abusive parents she moved to the east bay. She came to love the low hills there and how they turned colors with the season, green in winter, a warm brown in summer. When she lived in Alameda, she liked hearing the foghorns as well as listening to train sounds which faded off into the far horizons at night. She told me how she loved the wind, even as a child. She said it was like a toy the world gave to humanity for free. She told me stories about how she played with it and it, it seemed to her, played along. It could whistle tunes around corners, make music with chimes, fly kites and worked to sail ships. I've always loved the wind just as she did when she was a child.

I was born in 1973, August 16. Summer is my favorite season because of the free time and I like to go swimming. Autumn is next because of how trees change colors and all the holidays, especially Halloween. I am good at pitching a baseball. I am a good reader too.

3/14/84

I am naming my diary Joey. There is a long story there, my first best friend forever, back in New York, was George Napier, but he liked being called "Lil' Joey" after his uncle who was a great "coffee table" magician. He could pull all of his tricks out of his pocket or small valise and do them right there, on a coffee table. He was also very funny but I moved away when dad died. Later on, when we first moved to California, there was Alfred Parish, he and I liked singing, we met in music class in second grade, his nickname was also Joey, only I never asked why. Then after he moved away a new kid moved into his house. He was really named Joey and we became partners. We used to play all the time but now he too moved away, far away and it was done all of a sudden.

I only found out after he was absent from school for a few days and I asked his teacher about it. I had been feeling something odd in my heart every time I thought of him. Then, one night, I saw in a dream, his dead eyes and was so scared I went into my parents' room and they let me sleep alongside them. I never told they why but I couldn't sleep and was sick for a couple few days, as I remember.

I used to dream with Joey. We would go to play in our dreams. He said he dreamt of me too; it was our forever ever secret. We swore on it. Sometimes, we would talk about the times we had in our dreams together. It got such we could not tell whose dream was whose. I sure wish Joey were here. He taught me basketball and handball. He showed me how to catch lizards, snakes as well as other small animals out in the hills. He got good candy and movie money by selling them to other kids. I'd not do such a thing now; most kids do not know how to take care of them. Some feed them one time, let someone do bad things to them, or put them in a jar only to forget all about them.

Today, mom was on a tear and when she cleaned my room, top to bottom, she found my diary. I'd put it way under my bed. Although she told me it was ok to have, she cautioned that Vince would not understand. I knew, from the way she said that it was something that would make him angry. I think it's because he writes real sloppy – even I know he cannot spell or talk the way my teachers say one should. My mom would not say that, of course. She said he is my stepfather; he likes being right all the time. She tries hard to not get him upset. She made me promise to keep it hidden. Now I keep it in the space under the bottom drawer of my dresser and I won't even tell HER about that.

Tim says to write every day. I will not. I do not want to use up the pages faster than it would take to save for another book; I did the math, believe you me. I am already starting to save up for the next one. I guess I will say goodnight to you diary, goodnight Joey, see you in my dreams.

The Entries:

3/18/83

Dear Joey,

It feels good to write to you. You understand about all the dream things or ways. I wish you were here. Do you remember the colors? You know I still like to go to them whenever I can. When I cannot, I will still go to a quiet place not somewhere far off but away from people, their houses – all to just sit down, face into the sunlight, and listen to the sounds of the world around me. It could even be traffic, the other kids playing, or the sound of the wind. I like it when the wind brings things, the smell of wild flowers, somebody's barbecue, the scent of lightning in the air, grass, or piles of leaves burning – you remember. I know you do.

Do you know what happened today? I wanted to show Tim about the colors, dreaming, or going to the stars. He did not get it, not even one teeny-tiny bit; he just laughed at me then ran off. To make it worse he told the other kids. Now they make fun of me. I trusted him. Now I do not have one friend, really. Already, in a few weeks time, the bullyboys think I am weird. Now Tim is "in" with them, nice. I was going to show him how, up on the roof, it is so quiet you can hear much better. When I am up there, Vince thinks I am not home. I wish we did not have to move as often as we do. I am always new everywhere. I sometimes go under the house, through a break in the foundation. I stay there beneath the flooring. I dug a hole and I can sit under there; it is the coolest place on a hot, muggy summer day. It is like a camp where I read by candlelight. I wish you were still around. We moved to this stupid place when Vince got a job he likes. Ever since mom married Vince, we have moved a lot. Mom says he has to go where work is. Now we live in Alamo. It is a small place not at all like Oakland. There, in a crowded city, I could be the way I wanted to be. I could hide out in the open while being myself. This place is different – everyone looks at everyone. There is no hiding place. We are in a sub division with about 400 houses. It has its own elementary; it is bad – everyone knows everyone.

Vince got a bonus. He took us all to see a movie. It was about World War II, a battle in the Pacific war, Midway. Seeing the film made me want to read about it. Vince promised to get me a book on it. I like history. I want to know why wars happen as often as they do. In school all we seem to learn about are dates or places. I want to know about why they happen; maybe things will balance out, I guess.

3/19/83

Dear Joey,

Today at school I was staring out an open window when the breeze came in. It was quite hot in the classroom. The teacher was talking about a story we had read. I did not like the story. I looked out the window, closed my eyes then suddenly I felt cool all over my face. It was so nice. The smells of all the trees were around me and, I promise you, I could hear a stream, even smell water. I know there is no stream for miles around. I started imagining where the stream was. I looked for it in my head; you know the way we used to do in order to find lost things like we how we helped find that kid one time or pets. I followed the wind's direction to the stream. Birds were singing there; it was quiet. The sun was out. I closed my eyes. It was calm and warm. You remember how we used to feel like we were afloat and drifting, yet seeing some place we read about?

Well, that's when I heard the teacher calling me. I had to come back. I did not care, except the whole class was staring at me. I knew I was in trouble for "disappearing" again. When I said I did not understand the question, the whole class busted into laughter; she got mad – first at them, then she glared at me. I had to see her after school. When I did, she went on talking and talking. All I could think about was what would happen if I got home late enough that Vince would notice and then get mad. It would be worse, far worse if she called – I knew I'd get beat on. So, like you said to do, I prayed and wished and wished and prayed all while I looked like I was listening. I kept on going back to the stream too, I became disoriented, confused when, through the open window, such a bluster came! All the papers in the room started swirling around as books fell off shelves along with everything else. She raced to slam down the windows. The teacher got even more upset – but not at me – so I hopped to and really helped her tidy up. I guess she forgot about calling.

Vince was mad when I got home anyway – even though I was not too late. Like usual, I peeked to see him, if I could, before I went in; he had real mean face. He was scowling at the TV. The front door was open. I stood there a while before I rushed in. He yelled for me to stop. I only hesitated. He was bleary-eyed drunk. He snapped into a growling rage, got up quickly only to slip and fall, twice. I ran for it. He managed to collar me before I could get down the hall. He had a hard time keeping a good hold on me as I squirmed twisted or turned as he tried to smack my face "… don't you try to steal a march on me … boy."

I was fending off his clumsy blows when my mom came up behind him hollering, grappling at him and he started struggling with her. When I tried to move he lifted me up with one hand and shoved me into her with such force she nearly fell over as he bellowed, "If you don't take care of him I will." He went back to the TV, snapped it up to full volume as he sloppily bellowed, "I hope I can watch something for once in peace with G.D. quiet around here!"

She took me up. We cried silently as she carried me to their room. She whispered Vince had lost another job. Next she slammed the door behind us. Her nice face turned real mean. She told me through clenched teeth – if I did not cry or howl she was going to beat me for real this time. I screamed. She yelled and banged things around before she went out, slamming the door. He began to yell at her just as she did at him; they yelled over each other. It was grim. This went on until they left – still loudly angry. He never even asked why I was late. Later, at night, when the phone lines went down due to a freak windstorm. I considered it a lucky break.

Before I woke this morning, I dreamt I was playing a musical instrument, a flute of some kind. I did not get a chance to go to the library to find a picture of it. There was not enough time, since I had to read what I missed in class. I promised the teacher I'd always read the stuff. She said if my tests were ok, she would be ok. Joey said he'd help which always makes them easy as pie.

3/21/83

Dear Joey,

Today is Saturday. I've the house to myself. Vince is out looking for a job. Mom is visiting one of her "chatty" friends. I have to stay home since the phone man is coming to put in a new phone. I am supposed to let him in.

Saturday is the best day of the week. I take in the mail, the paper, and then get to watch all the TV I want, as long as I get my work done. Since no one was home, I took my diary out to reread it. It has only been a few days. I like to look at it; it is one thing that is really mine, no one else's.

It would be nice to write out in the open. Sometimes I wonder about the whole universe. I read a book about stars. It said stars are different sizes and colors. I found out the sun is bigger than the Earth. Who would have believed it? I asked mom; she said it only looks small because it's far away.

Vince came home. He had been drinking and went ballistic as soon as he closed the door. Maybe it was because dinner wasn't ready and he'd forgotten about going out, I couldn't understand that part. Also, she wasn't dressed well enough. She opted for being really patient and it worked although they mumbled arguments all through a "left over soup special." When I asked to be excused, he got mad at me. When mom told me to go, he got mad at her. He swung back to hit me. Mom grabbed his arm. He turned, roaring, and slapped at her a bunch of times though not so hard since she was yelling, "I'm working now, please, don't bruise ... don't bruise!" He froze, blinked twice, as if waking up, then they argued for a long, long time before getting quieter and, after a while, I could hear mom crying. That's another kind of thing that happens. I do not see why she stays with him. I opened the window in my room. I felt the peaceful quiet of the cool air. The breeze was soothing me. It was smooth and gentle. Everything got nicely quiet. I went to sleep.

3/23/83

Dear Joey,

Guess what happened today. It was great. We had a nice substitute. I got up in front of the class to talk, everyone had to. We all took turns. First, each of us thought up four subjects. We wrote each of the four on a card, put those into a shoebox, and, before our turn, we had to pick a card out of the hat. Some were scared. They spoke in a whisper or couldn't even look up. One girl cried so she got out of it. Some talked about dumb things. For example, Jeff Walker talked about light bulbs. I talked about imagination. I told a couple of stories I had made up. I made everyone laugh, even the teacher. She applauded. She whispered I was the best. This was the first time I had a joyful lift to my heart since about ever and it was at school yet already!

Coming home was not good. Like most always, I approached with my "ears on." I first looked through some windows. I could not tell mom about what had happened. She seemed upset. Vince was watching TV. I stayed in my room until dinner reading a science fiction story set on Mars. It was a fun sort of thing even though I knew Mars had no cities, dragons or canals. When I heard the door slam; I knew Vince had gone out and so I felt safe to come out.

I saw her at the kitchen table chopping vegetables. She was humming. I told her about my speech. She was glad; I could sense her heart was in what she said. She said Vince did not leave because he was angry; he was in a hurry for a quick job. I helped her make dinner. We ate while watching a Jerry Lewis movie on TV. I fell asleep before Vince had got home.

I am leaving the window open now. I want to smell the breeze, hear all the sounds and much, much more – it is so nice, so peaceful. I always hope for a happy dream.

3/24/83, Moving

Dear Joey,

Well I found out what they fought about. We have to move out of this house. We cannot afford it. Vince found a place which mom does not like; she says I won't have a room, which made me sad then angry. I am not going to say anything that might make him mad though. I decided I am not going to talk to him since it nearly always gets him angry. I will try not to let him see me; it makes him angry too. I am going to ignore or avoid him as much as possible. We are going to move within this week. I will be going a new school and I will take a bus most of the way to it.

I asked mom to help me keep my diary safe. She said she would put it in with her things. At least I did not have to worry about that. After dinner Vince gave me some boxes. We went into my room to pack stuff. I could only take school stuff. I was scared. All I said was "yes" or "no" when he held something up. I did not say more than those words; he did not notice. I think he liked it. When we were done, he looked at me in the funny way he had which had my tummy feel woozy. He stood there, I guess, waiting for me to say something. I had those scary feelings going on so I said nothing. Oddly, he turned around, left shutting the door behind him with a bang. I took the hint and stayed in my room. All I could hear was the TV playing until I slept.

Joey, will you come to me in my dreams? Was it you last night? You seemed very far away. I opened the window. I went to sleep listening to the sound of wind in the trees. There were some birds too. I dreamt of a far away mountain, a desert as well as a place with large rocks scattered on a grassy plain, which seemed to go on forever no matter how far or fast I flew over it.

3/28/83

Dear Joey,

I could not write for a long time. You never know how much you have until you have to move it all. It took three days to move across town. It was longer before I could get my diary. The small place is built on a hillside. The garage is below the living space. There are 17 red brick steps up to the front door, which admits to a small foyer. On the opposite side, and slightly to the left, you can see the entry to a hallway. As you look into it there is an open doorway on the left to the kitchen while, a bit farther on the right the bathroom's door. Farthest along, at the end, is the door to their bedroom, which also has a large walk-in closet and the door to the back yard. To the left of the front door is an archway leading to the front room, which has a nice set of windows facing the street. It also has a fireplace. I sleep on the sofa in there and have a nook behind a set of bookshelves where I stay out of sight. From the living room, through another archway, there is a cute little dining room and, from there, through another open doorway, you can enter the kitchen. The kitchen has a pantry all along one wall and, under the sink, behind a pair of little fancy swinging doors, is where you put garbage and recycling containers. This would be a good place to hide. The kitchen also has an outside door leading to a set of old, creaky, wooden stairs that go down to the garage side door. Now I keep my diary in a hollow space inside the box spring of the sofa bed's back. It is safe there. This house is far away from the part of town where all the stores and playgrounds are. I do not know anyone here so, after school, I stay quiet and keep to my tiny nook. Mom likes the quietude, Vince likes the rent and I like the trees not far from the back of the house and the open fields beyond.

Vince keeps getting drunk. My mom cries when he's not around and she thinks I am out. Even sometimes, they hit each other but not real bad, like Jamie's folks; remember how his mom went to the hospital sometimes? I mean before they moved away which was after she went in and stayed for that long time!

This new school is dumb but it's all a good thing, really. I find it more interesting to close my eyes looking at the colors or those far away places we had visited. This teacher is just as glad I do not need her attention, cause absolutely no trouble, and just do my work. The class is full of brats and noisy; they, apparently would just as soon leave me alone, unknown, and ignored as long as I just shut up and gave no smarty-pants answers or anything and I'm happy to oblige, Joey does the work when needed so I do not answer questions. One of the kids says it's a very good thing I don't have a nickname.

Joey, I am going to go and look for you. I made up my mind and I am going to do it – in every dream or nap. I know I will find you. I will leave to be with you – it will be like old times.

3/30/83

Dear Joey,

I hate Vince. I wish he would go away, never come back, or just plain die. If it did not hurt mom I'd find a way to get him real good. He has stared taking vitamin pills with mineral capsules. I found rat poison in the garage so I can get him.

It was an ordinary boring day at school but all day the teacher seemed to watch me. Anytime I almost got away, she called on me. Since I am in school she can always call on me. Then I have to decide how wrong my answer was going to be and then pretend I did not understand her explanation. I just do not want a note home; that would be the worst.

Tonight, as I sat at the dinner table while mom and Vince were finishing up in the kitchen, everything seemed nice. They had told me to wait so I sat quietly at the table. I did not do homework or nothing; I sat for the longest time and this great vision came; it was of one of the ancient cities in the secret place Joey talked about. Joey was calling me; he was there. It looked exactly like he had said. At first it was as if I were a bird or in a plane far above. It was great. I knew you were near. All I had to do was float on down.

Then BAM! Vince slapped me so hard I fell out of my chair and sprawled on the floor, my head hurting, and my right ear burning. He bent over me yelling as he punched at me two more times, real hard. I rolled out of the way once and his fist cracked into the floor, he howled. I did not know what was going on. I was still seeing the place far, far away but his fat, greasy face covered a big part of the sky – there was lightning striking all over. Screaming, mom jumped onto his back, grabbed him around the neck and began writhing her body to pull him off. He stumbled back and didn't get in to many good hits after that. I ducked down and scrambled under the table before he could hit me with a small frying pan. Roaring, he threw the chairs aside; I scooted off. Mom got between us. She held him back. I had not replied to him when he asked me something. He said he "wasn't going take such kind of crap from a snot nosed little brat." While she blocked him, I ran into kitchen, up the hallway, through their room, out the back door into the yard. I hid behind the old broken barbecue. I was ready to run through a break in sagging old fence. They were yelling and then I heard the front door slam, three times. I knew he had gone out. I waited until she called me in. I went to bed; that was my day.

4/1/83

Dear Joey,

Vince was sorry. I told him I had been thinking about a school problem. He is always willing to believe me when I say something about school; it is an easy lie. I do not care if I lie to him or even to mom anymore. If I had told him what I was doing, he would get real mad. I did not want that to cause mom to get upset. I've to help-out as best I can. I do not know why we do not get along; all I can do is take care not to cause any kind of problem and do the best to clean things up, and get them to laugh, yup, I can still do that, sometimes.

Joey where are you? We used to travel to far places anytime, now I get lost.

I got in trouble in school again. This time I was in the playground. Some big new kid started teasing me about my clothes. This was right after school was out as everyone was going to the buses or bike racks. I was on my way to talk to my teacher about daydreaming again. He started following me making fun of my shoes then laughing about the stripes on my white socks being different colors. I kept on walking as he kept on following while blabbing. I could tell some other sniveling tag-along brats came too – I heard their footsteps. Finally, as I turned around to tell him off, he grabbed me by the shoulders to toss me onto the ground but I grappled with him. Just as I opened my mouth to holler for help, or curse him, a powerful gust of wind caught him. He spun around and lost his grip on me before noisily slamming into a set of lockers. He collapsed into a heap. He was knocked out. I got scared when everyone said I did it. I got in trouble again. They called home. I was scared when I saw Vince walk in to get me. The principal explained how fighting is not allowed. He said even though the other kid was a known bully and witnesses said I had not started the trouble; Vince was supposed to talk to me. I dreaded it so much I did not say anything. Outside, Vince smiled for the first time ever as he told me I had done good to defend myself so well. He was proud of me – weird.

4/3/83

Dear Joey,

I should write one hundred times, every day, "School is boring" because it is, yet saying so would waste space so I'll never say it again. The only one worthwhile was Mr. B., from way back in second grade. He was the best. There was no one like him, ever. He told weird stories that had morals and were really real, I checked a couple of times. He taught us chess, how to sing, play music and made learning games, man! I paid attention like a laser.

I bought a ball with money I earned selling a snake. I knew the kid was into science so he would be good to it. Now I've a genuine Spaulding, which is the best for handball. I like playing though Vince will not play with me, even though he always gets excited about football on TV. He never does anything except tell me to do some job around here. Mom made a nice dinner tonight. It was very, very good. It was aromatic rice with fish, garlic, with Italian cheese on top.

I enjoyed it when we quietly watched a movie on TV. Vince was drinking sodas; he treated everyone. During the movie, he put his feet up on the coffee table. I could see how badly the heels of his shoes had worn and the souls were thin. He took of his shoes, crossed his legs, and set them on the coffee table. His ankles were set, one over the other, so his big toes pointed to opposite sides of the room. He did not know I was watching him as much as the movie. During a commercial, he took of his socks and dropped them on the floor; they stank. He started rubbing his toes and waxy, yellow, crumbly stuff fell off them. I could see these gross bits fall on the coffee table and the floor. He also had a blister on his foot. He stared rubbing on it at it as video played. Finally, he reached down and pulled off the skin. He put it in the ashtray. My mother looked at him with a sick look on her face. When he looked at her, she had already turned her face away and was coughing. I knew she was scared. She seemed to gag then almost said something but instead she stood and silently left the room. He was after her in a New York second. They went into their room where they began to argue and yell. I watched the movie. By the time it ended, they were just angrily talking. This is a good example of how they do things. He does something, or she does or doesn't or I do or do not – and it's bam, an explosion. Like always, or many times, later on they are talking quietly and they might drink a bit, laugh or talk happily.

4/5/83

Dear Joey,

I think mom is trying to make Vince talk to me in a friendly way. I do not care; I do not have to do anything I do not want to and I do not want to like him at all. I talk to him as little as possible. I can get away with very little as long as I tell him I have to study. Mom sees all this; I've seen her looking at me when I avoid saying anything to him. Like today, when he asked me about the stars and the sun. He knows I read books just as I knew mom set this talk up. I told her I had read stars were different colors and sizes so when he started in I had to play it close to the vest; warily I did converse admitting that I like to think about them since we are reading about them in school. I made sure I did not sound too interested and kept my part short — nice sure, but short. He seemed to try, a bit, but after about five minutes looked over to her, shrugged and asked me if I wanted to watch wrestling with him, I said sure, after I was done with homework. That was it; I went back to reading and he to his stupid old TV. Now I did not want to talk – even to mom. I know how to be quiet and that is my new approach, well that plus making trouble for him.

Oh, I do what they tell me to around the house though I do not have to do anything else. I put the salad oil in the refrigerator with a loose top and leaning just right so when he opened the door, it flopped over and gurgled a spill all over the extra big and very special coconut cream pie he'd bought for his friends to snack on, boy was he ever mad; he kicked the refrigerator so hard he hurt his dumb old foot and limped the rest of the night. When he is asleep or drunk I steal change. I avoid answering the phone and reset how loudly it rings. I let air out of one the tires on the car a few times. He thought it was a slow leak and got real mad when, after he took it in, the place couldn't find the leak. He decided to replace two tires. Joey laughed so hard I almost smiled when he was talking about it; I never got caught. Other times I reset the clock so it was off ten minutes one way or the other then I'd fix it before anyone knew only to reset it again. Joey and I sure can cook things up, like taking the sticker off the license plate—that was rich, he lost a job because he got stopped. Mom says even she doesn't know the worst of that one.

Joey, it was fun last night. How did you know where to find our old houses? It sure was nice looking at the old house from up in the tree as we used to do but I don't like the way the stream is being rebuilt into a flood control channel or the hills above it made into quarry, or some kind of mine operation. I have to grow up fast, be independent, and be able to do what I want to. I want to travel and explore. I've to get out of school.

I want to go flying in dreams with you. I don't know why you will not take me to where you live now. I get scared when I think about it; that's why I do not ask. I will never ask. I will wait for you to tell me.

4/6/83

Dear Joey,

I went to the store to buy groceries for mom. She was in the kitchen making some kind of pie for Vince; he had said a couple of his friends were going to come over. She could not go to get it herself; she had a lot to do. I volunteered. I figured I had to get used to going to the store if I am going to move out when I grow up. She told me exactly what she wanted and gave me enough money.

I did everything right, even made sure the change was correct. She made the pie. She told Vince I had helped. He did not even hear what she said; he was too busy with his friends, drinking and getting all loud and braggy playing cards. I stayed in the bedroom while they had fun in the living room. I read a book about Tibet and China. It mostly had pictures of mountain people in colorful dress; it was good enough for me; like they say, one picture is worth a thousand words.

I feel good these days. Vince does not bother me much at all. I guess my plan is working well enough. You know, every once in a while I can hear you when you talk to me – right inside my head. I guess either you cannot hear me all the time or very well in such a way as that.

I remember the first time I heard you came soon after Vince started showing up a lot and was almost living here. We were eating breakfast and you started in so very loudly because you were so happy to see me, finally, but I jumped out of my chair I was so shocked. I couldn't understand what you were saying I couldn't pay attention because Vince instantly glowered darkly, twitched a move, as if he was going to hit me, but froze – knowing mom was there. He was good at pretending; lying, and she believed he was just startled and annoyed. Mom looked at me funny. I told them I remembered I left a book at school, in the gym. I quickly added I had borrowed it from a friend and was afraid I had lost it. Mom soothed me by telling me the janitor probably found it and it would be OK. Vince just said, "Don't expect me to pay for it."

4/8/83

Dear Joey,

Today when I was listening to you, I did not hear what Vince was saying and he got mad. Parent teacher conferences are coming up and now I worry that both of them will learn how I "drop out" at school. Sometimes my teacher tries to talk to me about my friends. I will not tell anyone about Joey because I'll get big trouble and Joey says he'll go a far, long way away. I was stupid when I told her I was not able to listen, which is the truth though not the whole truth. Now she says she is going to write a note for a doctor. It means more trouble, which I do not think I could have avoided – it was inevitable. Hey how about that? I used a big word I learned today. I know if they get a note, Vince will get mad, especially if money is involved or if it troubles him in any way – which almost everything I do does. Mom will try to understand, which will hurt my heart. I cannot tell her about Joey, she'd tell Vince, the teacher, or a doctor. I've to do this by myself.

We had to do a painting today in school. I like watercolors; washes are fascinating. We were supposed to give the work as a present to our moms. I did not want to do it; such like things could enrage Vince but, since we had to write what our mom said, I cautiously brought it home, hiding it outside until I knew I could bring it in. Since Vince wasn't going to be home for a while I showed it to her and she liked it a lot. We talked for a while. She wanted to put it up on the fridge but we heard the car pull. I'm glad you gave me a warning because something sounded wrong with our little trick of putting a magnet tied to a bolt, a simple thing really, that only makes noise at certain speeds — which we also put in and take out. I get a laugh because its been driving him nuts. So, when mom went to the door, I took my artwork off the table and hid it. You saw the look on her face as she turned away, hesitating, but shrugging before deciding to meet him at the door. When he hollered at the damn lock, she froze; figuring how to handle what was coming. I bet she was going to be so distracted by whatever was wrong with Vince that she wouldn't think about my artwork, or me. I hid it under the sink and behind the recycling bin. I felt good about doing this.

Moments later, when mom opened the door, they immediately got into a shouting, throwing things, and slapping kind of fight. I hid. I want to go away. How many times can I say it and still have it not come true? Joey this is not fun at all.

4/10/83

Dear Joey,

When I came home from school mom had put my picture on the refrigerator. She put it in a beautiful paper frame. It was amazing; I do not know how she found it. I knew I would have to take it down; I do not want him to see it. I got lucky though when he came home. They decided to go right back out. They were talking about an evening out so I knew they wouldn't be back for a good long while and be drunk, fighting or both when they came back. I took the thing down. They came back very late, drunk and laughing. She never ever noticed it was gone.

From my diary, I notice a pattern for mom and Vince. They go from being very happy and laughing a lot about nothing, to being quiet and bored or silent until one of them, usually Vince, gets mad at something then they fight until one of them goes out for a while. After a while they'll talk for a long time or go out together before getting back to being all happy or romantic. I think they drink too much. He is always drinking beer; she likes wine. They both like the whiskey. One of the kids at school says his parents drink so much sometimes he comes home only to find one, the other, or both of them laying out on the sofa or snoring in an easy chair with their breath all stinky. He told me that's when he steals change and even orders pizzas. I know you should not drive when you drink so my mom, and Vince, must be very lucky so far.

It was good to see you again Joey. Was that China we went to? It was exactly like the book I got from the library. The big wall built a long ago and the way they write by making little pictures. I think it is a better way to write some kinds of things.

4/12/83

Dear Joey,

I don't like school, no one does. I don't write about the name-calling, teasing, or being pushed around – it isn't too bad; mostly everyone ignores me. I can hide right out in the open it. Today I almost got beat up. A teacher, one I do not like, fat, old "buffalo butt" Mr. Gondle, stopped it.

You see, this new kid, who was way big, ugly and incredibly and vastly, grossly fat – not to mention very, very ignorant, got into five fights his first three days. He won handily each time so he is number one now. He's got five snotty hangers on and these do what he says, imitate him, and mock his victims whenever he puts them under threat. He is so stupid a second grader can cap on him; I saw it happen. He does not speak clearly, curses a lot, and does poorly in class. When I saw him approach, I ran, easily escaping him while he huffed and puffed chasing me. I forgot about his "homies" though. They came from different directions. This was a planned attack. I was forced first one way and another until I was trapped behind the auditorium near the gym. When I turned to face his boys, a stiff breeze blew dust into their faces. While they coughed and sputtered, I ran through them. As I ran past a dumpster, the monster, who'd been clever enough to plan this interception, grabbed me by the collar and spun me around. His bloated sweaty face became even more horribly ugly as his smeary smile expanded, showing bad teeth and gums, plus horrid breath, jeez! He grabbed hold of both my upper arms in a painful grip. I got into a rage; I couldn't see straight. I kicked at his legs, he laughed. Then I kneed him hard in the balls. He dropped me, bent over clutching his crotch, and hollered. Then I stepped back, wind milled my fist to swing it up as hard as I could and the back of my fist smacked him in the nose. He yowled, staggered back, but still managed to snag my jacket as I tried to out flank him. By then the others were closing in from behind. He pulled me to him and got a chokehold. I kneed him again but missed his groin. He did not let go. Instead, he pushed me over, clambered on top of me and was trying to put a chokehold on. That's when Mr. Gondle happened upon us. Despite all the evidence, they held us both after school. I was hard scared all the way home as I tried to think up an excuse. I was thankfully relieved when I heard the record player blaring, shrill laughter, and loud voices talking over each other. They had a bunch of friends over and when I came through the open door I wasn't even noticed. It was another "party." Although I was glad enough about that, I worried all night about the school calling.

It was amazing to me yet it was like all the other times, I don't do anything! I never do! Yet I still catch hell. During lunch period, I eat by myself and simply wander around. I think in my head – maybe even talk with Joey. I try not to speak to him aloud since doing such like a thing would make me sound crazy.

So it was today, all I was doing was walking along by myself, thinking about painting my bike to make it look new; Joey was giving me advice, he showed me pictures. Joey knows I do not have enough money and that Vince will never give me more so Joey said I could weed lawns. All I needed was a couple of tools to be set. We had them in the garage. I was actually in a happy moment when "monster fat boy" started in on me.

It was over fast. One moment "the chunk" as his victims have come to call him, was towering over me in a screaming rage and the next he was grabbing his belly and blubbering. It looked as if something invisible had struck him hard in the belly. I saw his gut dent way far in. I was shocked at how he blanched and fell over, clutching his stomach. No adult saw it, so I was good.

I like having a diary. When I reread it, I can better see what is going on. I keep track of how often Vince gets mad and about what. Now I can see his blow-ups coming – though not all the time. Joey says I can write anything I want even about him. At first, he was mad when I showed him but then he liked it a lot, the same as I do. Joey is always my friend. We are always together, even when I dream. He says I can write what he says, if I want to. One time I was laughing at what he'd helped me write and mom came over. I ditched my book because I didn't want her to see it. You see, she and Vince sound the same when they walk. I told her I remembered something a teacher said. I'd not be writing if it were not for you Joey.

4/14/83, A Big One

Dear Joey,

Last night they had a big one. I woke up. It felt like an earthquake. They were jumping around or banging against the walls. It was very odd since they were not yelling or screaming.

He had found her little bank of money and had been spending a lot of it for a long time. I heard her repeat "8,000 dollars." I could only hear him mumbling back, way drunk I guess. She came out and left by the front door. I pretended to sleep. He came out soon after. He left cursing as he slammed the door behind him. I guess he hadn't actually been working all this time. She didn't know he'd been taking her money. She found out when checks bounced and she went to check her "cash stash" He wouldn't tell her what he'd been doing or where the money went. It was bad; he is so stupid.

In the morning, they were still not home but I knew the drill. I got up, fixed breakfast. This time I made buttered toast, had cereal, and then took three pieces of fruit for lunch. I also cleaned up a bit. It's my way of taking care of them and I can do it ok. I do it whenever they get sick after a party night. The house was very messed up. Some of the little dishes she collects, or used to collect, were broken all over the floor. I had to put my shoes on before I walked around in their room or the hallway. I had enough time to sweep up, stand up the chairs and I made the front room, at least, look pretty darn good.

Then, since there was plenty of money scattered on the floor in their room, I took as much as I dared. I knew what I could get away with, really. I put it all in my green tin box, my "cash stash" which I keep behind a loose cinderblock in the foundation. Whenever I find loose change or get a chance to take money, even a few dollars, I always take a little. I still had an hour before the bus so I started walking.

They were in the living room when I came home and barely noticed me. They looked very tired or sick. The TV was on, but they weren't really watching it. They didn't answer when I said hello. My gut wrenched and I knew to get out of sight. They had a stormy fight; it wasn't to bad just yelling and a few broken things. They went out and came back drunk, happy, and laughing.

4/16/83

Dear Joey,

I looked in a big dictionary at school. It says people write a diary daily. I can't because of the way our house is; my place is out in the open. It takes some time to get my book out of its hiding place. If he saw, he would ask what I was doing or worse look in it. Joey says I do not have to do a diary every day. I could not write for the last couple of days as Vince was home. I am glad he has had some "bad luck" recently. "Someone" got into our garage and stole tools, twice. "Someone else" smashed his taillights and the phone has been on the fritz. I am a real help, right? Joey, you sure have some good ideas.

Although I wish I had my own room, I like sleeping on the couch right under the front windows. At night, after they go to bed, I open the drapes to watch clouds or star gaze. I open the window too though only enough to get a scent of fresh air. I like to look at the stars while refreshing night air gently smoothes over my face – so clean and cool. If the window is open too long I worry Vince will notice, come out, get mad and yell about the draft. Before I go to sleep, I've got to shut the windows and draw the drapes. I got caught one morning by mom. She thought I'd get sick. I think they should turn off the heat at night that way they wouldn't get so worked up about "heating the whole damned outside world." The air is different at night. It is quiet. I like to listen to the sounds or voices carried on the breeze. I can hear pretty well. At school, when they tested me, they were surprised. I could hear much, much better than normal. They had a special doctor come to test me again. I listened to Joey pretending not to hear all the things I heard before. The doctor was very annoyed as was the school nurse. I can hear some of the things in the night even with the windows closed. Joey promised to remind me to close things up before morning. I do not want to be spanked or yelled at again.

Update:

I had a close-call once. Joey had me close things up just before I heard the floorboards creaking, their door opening, and some very quiet steps. It was Vince. All he did was stand over me, softly grumbling as he looked over the windows. I was under my covers. Joey told me he came over and bent down to look at me – just inches away then tiptoed out of the room, but then stood just out of sight listening for any sound I might make. He did peek twice, Joey told me. I waited until long after Joey said it was OK to move. Even Joey was scared. I sure was glad Joey woke me up in time to close things up. Vince had been drinking more than a little bit so he was ready to be mad. I was glad he had to work early the next day. After he got up and left very early, I opened the drapes and windows to look up at the dawn sky with its fading stars.

Today, in a book, I read there are many stars such as our own sun. Scientists say some of them have planets. I got to thinking; maybe someone is looking back when I look up except neither of us knows it. I came up with the idea that space, no matter where it is, must be the same all the time, everywhere. How could it be different? It should not matter if it is as far away as I can imagine it to be – or if it is right in front of my nose. There is no difference. Nothing is nothing; it's always the same everywhere it is – it's also forever everywhere. Its all one piece, one thing; that's what I know. Joey says it sounds right to him.

Joey, one last thing, I get confused. Sometimes I am writing to you, or about you. It depends on something I do not understand. I hear a voice so I write down what it says. I know you understand. Sometimes it sounds like you. Sometimes it IS you. Sometimes I just do not know; it might be another me or some other voice even. I think it does not matter. I am glad you agree.

4/17/83

Dear Joey,

I had a good dream last night. Joey went with me like ever. We were in a dark room in a large stone building. Each room was gigantic with huge doorways. They were crowded with statues; some were monstrous, others fantastic or nightmarish, many were enormous. I asked Joey if this was a museum. He said it was, sort of. Then he added if adults ever found this place, everything here would be put into one of theirs. He said they would fight over all this stuff especially the little boxes full of rings or tiny carvings of men, women, and animals. He would not tell me where the place was. Most of the statues were of animals. Some were of people with animal heads, bodies and or tails. Only two of the statues were of people as people – a man standing with a woman. They were standing side by side, looking forward as they held hands. They were radiantly beautiful. Their dress and robes were dreamy. Joey said the whole place was part of a city, which was all way underground but still on the coast of a very shallow, calm fresh water sea. I knew there was no real light but, as in any dream, no matter how dark it is, you can always see just fine. When I mentioned that, Joey cracked up. He did not stop for the longest. We played with some of the little boxes. I could not tell what had been in many of them – maybe the time or decay had ruined what they held. Some others had jewelry like little animals, sparkly necklaces, and other things – like what my mom wears when she dresses up.

We had a good time until I had to get back to wake up. I know dreams cannot last forever. When I got back, it was just starting to get light – I closed the windows, drew the drapes then quietly wrote this down. If I can remember to get up this early, I could write everyday. Joey says he might wake me up if he remembers which is funny – both of us always forget many things. There were times like when I took a bath by myself and, when I got out, found I still had underwear or socks on. I am like that.

Every once in a while, when I talk to Joey aloud, I forget to look around. I then I hate it when someone who was walking near me gives me weird looks or points. Most of the time, I just watch the movies he shows me or I talk to him in my head and to anyone else it would seem that I'm just sitting there doing nothing. I forget everything outside though; this is when I do not hear someone who could be right nearby talking to me – and this is what gets me in trouble. I've not found a way to explain it to people so I can get away with it. Joey says never, never, never tell anyone about the movies or voices, the places, the flying, the seeing, the colors and the music, nothing! Ever!

4/18/83, Violent Vince

Dear Joey,

Another school day and another trash load of troubles. The teacher says I was not listening to her when she asked me a question. I did not answer until she called my name five times. On top of that, I did not know the answer so I listened to Joey. I said what he said to say, which made her look at me in an odd, kind of overacting and sort of funny way. I couldn't help but notice how everyone was dead quiet. They stared at me too.

After a moment I blushed deeply. Not only had I spoken in a language only the teacher knew, I got the gist of what I'd said, Joey couldn't hide that or his laughter at me. She glared. She said I spoke with the accent they used in her home village. She kept looking at me until the class got noisy and she had shake her head, clear her thoughts and get back to the lesson. Bad thing was she made me stay after school. She wanted to know where I had learned to speak her language. I told her I did not know, which was true; I did not. I could not tell her about Joey. She wanted to know more so I said the words, which popped into my head exactly as I heard them. She gave me a puzzled look then shook her head slowly before telling me to go home. I did not think I'd be late. I believed I had escaped once again, until I got home that is.

As soon as I walked in the door Vince grabbed me from behind, threw me down on the sofa and began a spanking I will never forget. He was cursing a blue streak. It could have been about what happened at school or something else for all I could make of his raving. I was scared he had found my money. Mom came home in the middle of it all and began yelling and grabbing at him. He kept on trying to spank me. We all fell onto the floor. He was cursing; she was screaming back. I got the heck out and hid as they began to a howling storm of a fight. It kept on getting worse. I could hear slaps, smacks, and growling then a shrieking, yelling cacophony before the front door slammed three times. I waited under the kitchen sink hidden behind its two little swinging doors – I did it right this time – I left the kitchen door to the outside open so he would think I had run off that way. I waited for a time; sometimes he comes right back in to apologize only to start right back up. I waited until I heard my mom crying. I carefully got out to sneak a peek into the living room. She was standing in front of the window. I saw the doorknob was loose. I guessed he had broken it. While he was gone mom told me my school had called. They told her what I had said was very bad even though it was in another language. I told mom I heard a man on the street say it. Since I knew my teacher spoke that language, I had only asked what it meant. I told mom I did not know what it meant, which was true. She burst into tears pleading for me to "be good" for her sake.

A couple of hours later a happier Vince came back. He told her we were moving to another part of town. He said this neighborhood was giving him "bad luck" problems. They both stayed in the kitchen and got to drinking, before their laughter began. This was followed by one of their specialties, the "googly goo-goo, cootchy-cootchy coo, make-up giggly-talk. I went into

the front room to do my homework. After they started laughing,
I went to sleep.

4/24/83

Dear Joey,

Well, I did not get to write Tuesday. They had friends
over to play cards. They all ate, drank while they watched TV. I
stayed away from them, out of sight anyway. I was good at
staying quiet. They allowed me to come out to watch TV but
they were watching a fight. Although I was clearly not
interested, mom wanted me to stay, so I did. The woman from
the other couple tried to be friendly. She asked questions, acted
silly and rubbed the top of my head. Vince told them about the
fight I'd had. When he told them what I had said, the man and
the woman howled with laughter. Vince looked at me as if he
liked me. A bit later, the woman came over, a little bit boozy-
woozy and thick with lots of mixed smells. She wanted to talk
about my friends. I began talking about Joey though not by
name. When she asked me for his name I got scared. Joey
appeared in mind; he told me to be afraid, very afraid because he
was.
When she asked about my best friend, I talked about a
guy I knew at school but, my intuition flashing, I decided to use
a different name and description. This always made it easier to
keep a lie like this going if I had some one real to base it on. I
told her I wished the house was bigger, that we had nice, large,
wild yard or that I had my own room. Joey says, when I am
older, I can have all of those things.
Mostly when they were smoking or playing cards, they
kept the window open. I could look for a long time at the stars
and cried knowing I'd never ever see them – I mean up close. I
dreamt of the wind taking me places or how, in my dreams, I
could go with it, laughing as it played with leaves or in clouds.
This simply made me sad all through. A tear rolled down my
face as I looked out the window. I was glad of the fresh smells it
brought in and that the stale, smoky air was leaving.
I was calm until that other lady came over again. She
asked me quietly, while the others were excited about the TV,
what was wrong. I didn't need Joey to warn me. There was

something about her eyes – even I could see it. There was the light, of course, yet it was glinted, sharp and cold – not sparkling, liquid, and warmly colored. She dried my eyes and held me. She seemed really nice. I almost told her something about Joey as she told me the stars were all very far away before adding that, in a dream, I could go to any of them. Joey told me she was right. That was the first time he ever agreed with any adult. It felt good. She was pretty too. My mom came over; I knew she wanted to know what was going on so I shut up. The woman looked at her. They stared at each other silently, I expected a fight, but my mom smiled nervously, looked down, and went back to the men. I wondered about this woman. Why was I suspicious of her, I mean besides her eyes. I think she suspected something about Joey so I was very careful with my lies. If I could not figure one, I'd shrug, get quiet or act sleepy.

After a while mom came back. They men wanted to go out for a nightcap. It was time for me to go to bed. Vince left the window open to air the place out. After they were gone, the house was quiet and cool; they could not blame me for leaving the window open this time.

I wish mom could be something like the other lady. Mom never seriously talks to me except some rare times such as when they've been happy for a few days, or he's not around for some reason. Lots of time she's on the phone or she goes "out for a little bit" or endlessly watches TV. Oh I do hear from her when I make a mess, how I am trouble for what I do in school or how I make Vince mad. I guess I need to be quiet. Maybe, if Vince would play with me, stop drinking, get a real job or do anything the other kids' fathers do, it would be different, but it's not different. It will never be. He goes to work, is always tired, not that would like to pal around with him anyway, he's a would be jock, sport's nut, card playing, dumbbell. He does not like me.

I remember one time at supper, when I asked her if she would read to me, she said I could read on my own. When I complained, Vince told me to shut up and when I complained about that he hit me. I hated him for that and her for a whole week when she did not do anything about it. Mom sometimes talks to me about the TV shows she sees, the soaps or how she worried she gets when Vince is driving big trucks or doing delivery work. I like it when he is not around although it never gets to feel normal as in the old days with my real dad. She didn't drink at all back then.

Sometimes I feel as if I am not here. I used to hide so she could not find me. Once, when I was sick, I stayed home from school and, to be real sneaky, I hid under the coffee table in the living room because she had put a cloth over it to make it look nice. I stayed there even when she called me many times. At first, she was angry thinking I had gone out to play and should have gone to school. As she paced around the floor I watched her shoes. Then the phone rang. It was one of her friends, and she got all giggly on the phone. I wanted to get out but she waited for him so I was still under the table when he came over.

They had coffee cake and coffee. Both of them yakked for a long time. It seemed endless. Mostly mom talked about how she hated the way she had to live or how Vince was not nice. I wondered why she never told Vince what she told this guy. The man said she should separate from Vince. She said she loved Vince; she only confided in him to get it off her chest, he laughed at how she said that; she laughed at that a lot. I wanted to cry; they seemed very happy together. My stomach was hurting. I began to feel all funny. It was Joey's idea to hide. He had promised me something special was going to happen. I wondered what kind of present it was since she had cleaned up the house, was singing, and had gotten all dressed up.

My plan had been was to surprise her before she could surprise me. However she started talking about how I am trouble, how she wanted to move away and leave me with Vince for a while. After that, I froze where I was. I heard them talking softly. She began giggling a bit. I heard her moaning and breathing heavily, like when she scrubs the kitchen floor or cleans the oven. She was panting faster. He was saying he loved her. She was saying it was good – so, so, so very delicious and good. It got quieter before they started making some regular noise on the sofa, breathing hard exercising. I kept hidden. Joey said it was important to keep awake but I fell asleep. I wanted to dream of all the nice things we would like to see.

Mom's scream woke me. She found me. She was very red faced and way mad. She yanked me up hard turning my arm and it hurt badly. She hit me, carried me over to the sofa, and threw me on it. She yanked up my covers and dumped them on top of me to cover me up. I cried hot and hard though silently. I curled up as tight as I could, calling, in my mind, for Joey. He did not come. All I wanted to do was surprise her. I heard her in the kitchen banging things about. When it was quiet, I got off the sofa bed to apologize. She was sitting in a chair as the man came out of her room putting on his coat. He seemed friendly. He left right away without saying much to mom and nothing at all to me of course. Mom said she was tired and told me to go to bed.

I do not care about all that. Thursday night was special. Joey and I had a lot of just plain fun. The window was open. I was looking out at the stars. A breeze settled on my face. I wondered where the wind comes from and goes to. Joey said he was sure it had to be everywhere. He said my breath was like a wind. I smelled pine tree just as I did when we went camping once a long time ago – before I before I knew Joey or the disaster that Vince was and is. I told him about the fresh air, the campfire smell, the deer and raccoons.

I was holding on to my picture of the deer to show Joey when I smelled smoke. I woke up, looked; everything was ok. I lay back down; again, there was the smell. It was so warm and wonderful. With my dream eyes, I was looking out the window. With my real nose, I sniffed for the fire as I looked to see where it was. The smoke was on the breeze. I whispered a wish to follow it. There was a wispy sort of murmur, whoosh – I was flying as a bird, except much faster. Soon the forests and mountains were far below. I saw a lake. On its shore was a single tiny light, a campfire. There was a family around it – a man, a woman, a boy, a girl along with their big, red shaggy dog. The dog tried to howl along with the song the dad was playing on an old guitar. He did it in a way so funny they all laughed as they sang different words at the same time. I loved looking at them. Their eyes were aglow with happiness. I drifted down to hover close when a breeze came up forcing them to scramble off to chase their things, which were blown around as the campfire struggled to keep going. I rose off, the breeze died down quickly. I went away much sadder.

I opened my eyes. I was looking up at the window again. It was almost dawn. I whispered, very softly, to thank the wind then, zing, I felt a breeze, which had me feeling glad. I was so happy inside I almost laughed out loud. There was a sprinkling of mist in the air, fresh as spring rain and a scent of the ocean, turned earth, the forest soil, the prairie, snow, autumn with the scent of approaching thunderstorms. I was the happiest I had ever been. Again, I asked to go. The wind softly rushed in through the window, it gentled about me with whisper soft touches. I closed my eyes and was off again to another forest – this one in a deep redwood valley. It was very, very quiet. I met up with Joey. We ran around playing hide-and-seek. I got dizzy, sort of, because of the strong scent of the trees. When I woke up, I could still smell it on me. I was scared mom or Vince would notice. They did not. Joey and I knew how to follow the wind. We believed we could go anywhere.

4/25/83

Dear Joey,

I had to could not write much yesterday. Mom sent me to the babysitter again. She likes to go out when she can to visit friends, she says. She never dares do such a thing if Vince is home; she always stays put, fussing at things around the house or watching what he wants on TV. The babysitter always has many kids at her place all the time. I get to play; I like that. Sometimes one of mom's guy friends comes by and we all drive over to the sitters in our car but it is always mom who picks me up, takes me for ice cream on the way home and always tells me not to say anything to prevent a "Vince-rage." No matter how uncomfortable I was about these trips I never, ever told Vince. Whatever floats her boat, as they say. What he does not know is his problem and mom's friends, sometimes, are hers. Vince does not like how she puts me away "like a piece of furniture." This is something else they have stared to argue about lately. Vince says she does not cook as much as she did before. He has yelled more than once, "If I want instant food, I could go out and get it myself." When I spoke up once saying I liked hot dogs, macaroni with cheese and Campbell's soup Vince told me to shut up and get out. I wish my old dad were here. Those were the good days when they both used to read to me, mom used to sing in morning as she and I worked together hanging out the wash or folding clothes fresh and warm from the dryer.

4/26/83, Danger and Co-dependency

Dear Joey,

Last night was fun in the mystic forest again. Now, since we know the way, we can go anytime we want. I liked the deep smell of the tall trees; the fun we had going into animal minds, taking over and playing with them, as them. I told you we could go inside them and become them the same as we can, in our living dreams. After we got back and you left, I went out again, this time to a beach. I played music with some other boys, drumming; this was in Africa I was in an African boy. I was confused when you had me wake up and wait; I was angry at first, I love it when I played music or sang in my dreams. After a minute, though I caught a whiff of smoke. I opened the window a crack. It smelled like campfire. I felt very joyful! I opened the window all the way. I had a hard time not laughing aloud. I smothered myself in the pillow and kicked all about to use up the happiness. I felt like going out and running for a long time. I saw that happy family again, only for a moment, but I loved it!

Then, I lay back to watch the stars and breath the gentle air. The scent of smoke faded as a smell a pine arose. When I closed my eyes, I could see the pine forest, smell water in the air, and my feet felt the chill dew on deeply soft grass. I was facing the open window when something touched my ear or whispered; it tickled like a butterfly. I looked; there was nothing. I closed my eyes; again. This time my other ear was touched and I giggled a little bit. I heard a sound like the ocean in a seashell something touched my neck; it tickled. Whatever it was; it was fun. Every time I opened my eyes to look around, the sound would vanish. I heard Vince grumbling. Afraid he might be getting up; I closed the widow before covering up and settling down to look like I was fast asleep.

It was a lucky thing too. Joey told me he came sneaking over to where I slept. I could hardly breathe or move. Joey said he stood looking down at me watching. I almost did not believe him until I heard Vince mumbling angrily, as he moved the curtains slightly to check the windows. For a while I heard nothing yet I knew he had to be there. I could smell his stinky breath through the sheet; he was that close. I asked you to pray Joey and we did. There was a rattling at the kitchen door and a banging sound. We heard his footsteps go into the kitchen. We heard bathroom noises before his shuffling footsteps headed to their room.

When I heard his first snore, we both knew it was safe to open up the window again. This time only clean night air flowed in. I imagined a fountain of glistening water in an ancient city somewhere. I closed my eyes and kept very still. Nothing happened. I kept on trying to go there until I fell asleep.

That's when you showed me some mountains. They were very far away and always have snow on them. Do you remember the part where we were walking along the roadway made of big stones? How we went off of it after while and that let us find the waterfall with water so deliciously sweet and satisfying. How could I've become as thirsty as I was? It seemed I could never drink enough. We took off our shoes and nipped right into a great swimming hole. We laughed a lot splashing each other after we had a chance to cool off after getting sweaty walking all those miles uphill. We swam for a long time, came out, and slept in the warm sunlight on the broad hot boulders. We dreamt all the rainbow colors that time, right?

When I awoke, I was still there. This had never happened before. I wanted to go home but I couldn't find Joey. I became scared. The sky was dark and grumbling louder and louder. The thunder began to roll in. Lightning struck out nearby. I was lost. I called for mom and you, Joey. Joey where were you? A giant storm broke. The wind and rain were so heavy they knocked me down. Things fell; I got hurt. The ground began to move. I screamed. I held on to a tree root. I believed I'd be ok if I could just stay with it. The storm howled; the lightning roared; the ground heaved. I shut my eyes tight. I held on until I was forced off. I was lifted, tossed about, shaken and hit repeatedly.

When I opened my eyes to look for the root, I was lying on my living room floor. The carpet was soaked – as was the sofa. My mom was pulling Vince away from me. They were fighting and yelling. Mom ran into their room slamming the door. He slipped and fell on the slick floor as he ran after her ran his shoulder into the door, which boomed. Then he began hammering on it until it broke off its hinges. He wanted to know who Joey was. I feared he'd found my diary. I wondered why all the water was here; it wasn't, hadn't been raining, well not here anyway. Still, that window was open. I knew I'd get the blame. I had bruises, my ribs ached and I had a giant headache. I felt sick. I threw up three times quickly getting dizzier each time and then my body kept on trying but there was nothing left to give. When I tried to stand I fell over – my legs were wobbly. Lucky for me they were still at it only this time they were throwing stuff, things were breaking and they sounded like animals. It wasn't even morning. The last thing I remember about the fight was long tearing sounds, like ripping cloth. I did not go look. I hid behind the sofa after opening the front door.

Just as quickly, there was silence. The wet curtains flapped against the wall. The quiet was thick with danger; I saw Vince or rather his shoes move around on the floor. He was drunk, went stumbling around in the kitchen yelling my name and banging things around. I heard the kitchen's outside door open; there was a clatter as some stuff fell and a couple things broke. It sounded like he fell. The draft he created slammed the front door shut. He ran back through the living room, bolted out the door calling my name and cursing all the while. I stayed hidden. Later, he came back and flopped down on the sofa. He was talking to himself in a crazy way. It made no sense even compared to the times Vince was regular drunk and did not make sense. He was slapping himself, muttering, banging the coffee table, sometimes getting up, and pacing for a few steps before slumping back down. I heard him crying. I had never heard the like. He went on and on in a disjointed way about how it was her fault, my fault, how the GD sofa was ruined, the rug water stained, the wood underneath was going to warp, and how the landlord would want "big damned money." He repeatedly asked about Joey. He went on about his lousy car, bad luck, missing tools, and how messed up things got after he was mixed up with her. He called me a little bastard. The floor where I was had water all over it yet I dared not move. He went out the again. There was a draft so I knew he left the door open. Lucky for me, the breeze got warm, then very, very warm. The part of the floor around me dried up. I got woozy then fell asleep. I knew I had bruises on my legs. My head had a good-sized lump on it too. I worried about going to school. I mean I could hide everything except for my face or head. I did not want someone at school to ask about marks or bad clothing or being sleepy or hungry. My usual lies were ready but wouldn't cover things up. I don't want more trouble. I didn't think an ice pack would fix the swelling in time for school, I thought about it.

I did not sleep long. Joey woke me as dawn light came through the window. He knew it was ok. I knew it was quiet. I got out from under the sofa then, as if a madman, I set first the living room, hallway and then the kitchen to rights. Satisfied that they looked good I remembered the bedroom.

However, every time I looked down the hallway to their closed door, I felt funny. It looked as though the walls were not at the right angles, the perspective was off or it was too shadowy. It was weird; I kept thinking my mom's clothes were in the room all torn up yet hovering around as if different invisible people were wearing them while dancing or floating. Every time I started to go down toward their room I could not make myself get closer than half way. I felt sadder and sadder with each step. Joey said he heard real weird bad music. I didn't. It also got colder and colder; I could see my breath turn to frost in the air. When I went past the halfway point I began to get the shakes and got a bit dizzy. It was bad.

I whispered, over and over, "Mom come on out, it's alright he's gone." I wanted her to wake up, to come out. I wished harder than anything for her to hold me and rock me until it was all right. I wanted her to sing again. I did not know what to do.

When the sun was well up, I decided to eat. I made sandwiches cheese, mayo, mustard and baloney with corn chips – my favorite. I ate them plus two bananas and a lot of milk. I was full. I still could not go down the hall so I sat in the big chair in the living room.

Just as I started to drift off, I felt a tickle at my ear. I looked around – there was nothing, not a bug or bit of spider web. It happened twice before I could settle into the chair. As I drifted off, something came again. There was a sound something like a seashell's imitation of the ocean, though there was more than an ocean's sound – there was a dreamy pulse to it, a pattern of hushes. I was curious. I relaxed, opened my hearing to its limit before sleeping deeply not keeping alert.

I had a waking dream but without Joey in it. I was in the kitchen making soup on the stove and I heard the usual squealing brakes of Vince's car out in front. Oddly, I wasn't afraid. The whole place looked great. I had fixed the sofa, dried out the rug, and cleaned the floor with Murphy's Soap; it looked new. I ran to the door and waved. He was in the car waving to me, all smiles. He got out and was standing beside it. He called me. I was so glad he liked me. I had done something right. I watched as I ran from the door toward him. The clouds were beautiful although crazily shaped like question marks. Then, just as suddenly as you change channels on a TV, instead of waving to me, he was screaming as grappled me and got his gnarly hands on my neck. I tried to scream but could only gargle a raspy croak instead. I had no voice. "I know about the damn bolt and magnet," he screeched. I watched as he threw me down, smacking my head loudly on the concrete. He choked me. I lashed out crazily and then, went limp limbed and still.

I felt dizzy. I began to float like a balloon. I did not care what he was doing to my body below. I floated over to where he was crouched over me. He let go. My head was bent all the way back. My eyes stared. They were glazed over, droopy and blankly stared.

In my dream I floated along with him as he went back into the house. I heard sirens coming. Why would Vince do this? The cop cars drove up onto the lawn. I saw them get out. When they saw me, they drew their guns. A couple of them went around to the back of the house. I heard momma screaming. There were gunshots. I woke up for real.

It was the next day.

The sunlight through the window was dazzling and I was shocked to see the clouds were like those in the dream. As I looked around I saw I'd cleaned the place pretty darned well. I felt good. Everything looked normal. I had fixed it all! I could not ignore the clouds however, they were just like in the dream; I decided to run away. I got my secret money, put lots of food

into my backpack with all the camping stuff I could take. I had
finished putting clothes into it when I heard his stupid old car
braking out front. For some crazy reason I walked carefully
toward the front door then turned on my heel, since Joey said so.
I peeked from between closed curtains. Vince was getting out of
the car as he called my name. He seemed happy but his smile
was the same as in he dream. There was a large package in the
back seat with a broad red ribbon on it and I remembered that
such a thing was in the dream too. He said he got a great job. He
had a big present for me – which it was something I always
wanted. He waited. I was about to second-guess my dream when
his face changed; it was as if a mask fell off. I could see his
animal rage before he got control enough and smiled again. I tip
toed to the back of the house, went out a side window, which let
me get down into a neighbor's back yard and jogged through
their breezeway to the street on the opposite side of our block.
The last I heard from him was his calling my name from inside
the house with his loud yelling voice. Mom screamed horribly. I
heard sirens approach. Police cars were close. I ducked down
behind a car parked nearby and wiggled under it to watch.

I could not go back, even with my mom's gargling
screams. I stopped up my ears. My heart was beating hard when
I heard him howling in pain. As the first police car arrived, I
walked away keeping low. I kept on going up into the hills
behind the house. I was watching from above when they began
to speak to him with a megaphone. A couple more police cars
arrived.

5/3/83, Away with the Wind

Dear Joey,

I could not write for days. Everything got wet from the
rains on Wednesday. I feel OK. I've my pup tent, two blankets
and it's spring. I made a mistake by sleeping out in the open
when it rained. Lots of things got soaked while I put up my tent.
My diary was ruined when it fell out of my pack and had been
left outside all night. I had to get another one with the money I
took with me and will recopy it. It was good I began writing in
pen, much of the pencil stuff is lost but I still have my memory.
Mom, in case you read this, I decided to leave a lot of stuff out

of this one. I've one hundred and eighty dollars with a big sack of change – pretty good!

I did not go back into town. I went all the way to another one, lots bigger with buses. This was Berkeley. Being from Alamo, I liked Berkeley a lot. I had a good time with some of the kids there, except I had to make up stories so I wouldn't have to tell them where I lived or anything – these kids are tricky, I have to say. I have to be very careful, especially when dealing with money. I played in the parks, talked to a balloon man and bought a hot dog, a big warm pretzel and ice cream. I liked riding the buses a lot.

When night came, I went back up into the hills. I feared people would start asking pointed questions, such as where I was going or staying. It took me three days to get a routine that I felt was trustworthy for going into Berkeley during the day and using a late bus to get back into the hills at night. I wondered if I should go somewhere else. On the fourth or fifth day I didn't get back till late. I had gotten into a really wealthy kid's birthday bash and I had to walk much of the way as the bus line, which was far away, and so I had to improvise.

Well by the time I got back I found that raccoons had gotten into my stuff so it was a real mess. I couldn't find a bunch of the coins I had stashed and was getting hungry. I thought about begging on the street, even at night; I had to get food.

Just after I had decided to trudge on down to see what I could find, I caught the scent of a pie – real delectable one. The breeze brought it to me. I followed it for a long way. The wind must be the greatest thing. If I could get the pie I'd not have to risk going into the city. I was afraid the police were looking for me since I was a runaway. The pie was in a window of an old farmhouse. It had been set out to cool. It was a great big one too and very hot. Before I could take it, I had to run back behind some bushes when an old woman came into the kitchen. After she was gone, I went back. This time I had my shirt off so I could wrap it around my hands. I ran off with the hot pie easily. When I cut into it, it was all vegetables, cheese and eggs or something like that. I waited for a long time until it cooled. I was surprised how much I liked it. It was real spicy and filling. It lasted two days. When it was gone, I had to go into town. I made sure to replace the pie pan with some money in it tied to a rock. I gave a twenty-dollar bill. It was worth it. I wrote them a note thanking them.

The first thing I did was go to a gas station to get washed up. I took a birdbath, as I did at home, filling up the sink and using a washcloth to clean up all over. Boy, it felt good. I went to a Double Load Laundromat to wash my clothes. A real nice lady showed me how to use the machines. I told her Joey was my name, which is sort-of true anyway.

5/3/83

Dear Joey,

I've to hide from the rangers in the park. It's easy to do as long as I do not make fires. I've a real campsite with my tent and a log outside for a chair. I moved a big flat rock on top of three small ones for a table. I guess I can stay here until my money runs out. I eat peanut butter, fruit, bread and sometimes salami and cheese. I've to eat cheese on the day I get it; it does not keep. I love granola; it keeps well. I fill up my canteen with water, add powdered milk, honey then shake it up and poof: sweet milk for breakfast cereal.

I can stay up here for days, months. I only spend a few dollars a week at this rate. I dream with Joey all the time and I always get to sleep outside with the wind and stars. I love it.

One night we dream flew into San Francisco. He wanted to show me what a real big city was like; he had been there before. We went all around; we saw many people in bars, looked right in their faces. They could not see us at all. There are many places I want to go see; maybe I will some day. There were more cars there than I ever saw in Alamo, for sure. We went to a few other cities where the language was as different as the people were. Only in London could we understand, sort of, they spoke like us there. We saw lots of castles, some with people still in them; they called each other Lord, Duke, or such a like things as that. I saw why, when it is night over here, it is daytime in London. It is because the earth is round so the sun can only shine only on one side of it at time. Joey and I went way out in space to see it for real.

In London, there was the biggest circus you ever want to see. We watched it all from the best seats, well through the eyes of those sitting in them. After a while, I got tired of looking at the horses all dressed up, the sad elephants as well as the acrobats or clowns. I took Joey out to a desert where lots and lots of soldiers were, not ours, someone else's. We saw a battle between big armies. We were inside a man as he ordered a jet shot down by couple of rockets. After it blew up, there were more jets and more firing. It was a war. It was horrible.

The best thing was right before I woke up. I was sleeping outside, hovering between waking and sleeping, lying perfectly still, before I open my eyes. Sometimes you can keep dreaming if you do that. Also, it's fun to imagine anything you want because it in that state of mind you can really see anything you give a thought to. So there I was listening to a couple of distant birds as well as the trees, when there was a whisper at my ear: "Hello, hello! You must get up and go!"

I froze, scared. I knew no one was there yet I could feel a warm breath on my ear. I could have slipped back into a dream. Joey said he did not know what it was, though, dream or no, he agreed we should go.

I got up, dressed, began gobbling an apple when I heard a jeep stopping on the road I knew was nearby, although I could not see it.

I rolled away the log and tumbled the over the stones before I jogged away. The breeze came up a bit blowing dust, leaves and twigs up and all around; it was the biggest dust devil I ever saw. It waxed after it passed me strengthening into something of a squall – all well behind me, thankfully.

Out of curiosity, I looked back – the clearing appeared as if no one had ever been there. The windstorm had reached the trees, which were all swaying in wild confusion. I turned to continue jogging away.

All day long, the wind was funny. It shifted around, sometimes making it impossible to go in one direction forcing me to either take shelter or change course. Since I did not want to stay still, I kept on the move through what seemed something like an invisible maze of air.

After a time, I saw a ridge; I made for its top. I wanted to see where I was. I had county and state maps. I hoped to fix my position. When I got to the top to look around, I had a good idea, from the mountain peaks and a highway, where I was. That's when I saw a line of rangers on the next ridge over. Even though they were close enough to give chase, it was simple enough to avoid them, as they couldn't see me yet. I headed off directly away from them. I only stopped when I came to an opening in the trees and saw that there was only open grazing land beyond the hills in that direction. A distant shout had me look in yet another direction. There, coming over a nearer rise, was a smaller band of rangers. I knew they would either close on me or pass darned nearby. I was afraid, not only of being caught. There was something else. The situation felt fearfully wrong. I took off running until I could not run any more. I could hear men's voices, still some distance off, approaching only now it was from three surrounding directions – I was boxed in.

Freaky scared, I hunkered down into a small clump of brush grouped at the base of a cluster of oaks. There was a storm brewing, just my kind of luck. The rangers were closing on me as the storm burst. It was a real downpour. I sneezed a few times. I worried about getting sick. I smelled the charge in the air before lightening struck the tree above me. Several branches broke off and fell harmlessly about and over me – making my hiding place even more secure. Not a few feet off, I heard a couple of men's voices passing by and, a few minutes later, another couple came by – though from another direction. These last two stood around for a while. After the rain got even worse, they decided to leave. I made the command decision to follow them since I did not know which way to go. Those men unknowingly helped me out. When they got to place where I saw housing, I broke off from them.

I ran again. I was happy. I knew those rangers were looking for me. Joey said they could be training. I almost agreed but Joey couldn't explain why there would there be so many just to find me. I walked all day only stopping at dark to eat. To be safe, I didn't use a candle or flashlight. I got comfortable, in a nice little copse of trees with deep soft leafy ground. I comfortably settled down. As I drifted off to sleep, there came a whisper. I could feel the breath at my ear, it said, "Waif, you're safe."

I dismissed it as a dream and began to fall asleep again. There came another whisper, "Hello … hello?"

I started, sat up and looked around. There was no one around so I asked, "Who are you?"

There was sudden gust of wind in the treetops before silence.

There was a smell of some animal, a drift of fog came then went. I grew sleepy. I lay back down yawning. I was very tired. Again, when I was nearly off to sleep, the whisper came. I was not scared this time though; I already knew there was no one near me. I considered it a puzzle. Maybe, this was some one else, like Joey, of course, trying to talk to me. I began to wonder. Curious I relaxed settling back to see if it would happen again.

Joey agreed all we had to was wait, be very still and not fall asleep. Again there came some whisper in my ear, like a hint of breath; I had all I could do to go stay still.

I heard as if from far, far away: " …nn … nly … t- lk … er-fect – ly sill."

I stayed as still as still could be and silent. Joey was ok. I knew he was as curious as I. He would not admit it though. He likes to think he knows everything.

And softly it came, "Ahm th w…nd, …atch … n…ee." With that, the whole of the canopy began to sway gently – with a rhythm. I got it; it was the wind. I was expecting to see some great figure with clouds of hair and big puffed up colorful cheeks the way they draw the wind in storybooks. All I saw were the trees swaying and clouds clearing off. I watched, staying as still as could be, as the swaying trees and their rustling leaves made something near to music – there were rhythms, certainly, as well as a shushing and whistle like whisper. Again, at my ear, came wispy words I could not understand. I heard them as one hears the moaning at eaves, the breeze in grasses or air in seashells or as a hint in a dream. It was all of these and yet again none.

I found I could keep quite still by staring a lone star. As my sight was dazzled and its light appeared to diffract into shifting snowflake-like patterns or shapes, the contrasting dark surround helped me focus with intent.

I whispered, "Why do I've to be so still to hear what you say?"

"You … I … m of, in air, through and through air and therefore everwhr and no – ere at … nce. And I mus … fin y – r ear … to concentrate … th' motions … trc ee. Easy … now easier if … you … ill … ee st … ill"

"Yes" I barely whispered.

"So I ca… …earn ow to llow you t ear me."

"You have to focus on the ridge patterns of my ears." This allows my hearing to get the vibration, clearly I had moved too much. I waited.

"Yes, you learn fast that's best, yes." Already I was thinking a thousand things. I liked the way it said 'yes', the 'Y' sounding much like a soft 'F' with the rest nearly inaudible except for the clear sibilant 'S' tailing off and fading up as if in question. It was the Wind. I always enjoyed the wind at my house at night or at the beach. I always felt it was beautiful. I felt safe and, for the first time, not at all worried.

"I don't understand how you can talk." Now I was hardly moving my lips to make sounds, so that, I could be as still as I might.

"Birds … all animals … sound … how do you make words?"

"Well, I am a person. I've always had a mouth, lungs, tongue, and everything. You don't have those."

"Clearly I do not need these, if you please."

"How come no one has ever heard from you before, I've never read of anything like this."

"I am in your stories and songs. There are many ways to play with the hands of fate to affect rights or wrongs. There are many things which were never written, many things from records smitten; or whispered as slips from the lips of those who, as they died, let truth get out or lied, though such were not heard for what they meant no doubt. You have heard of ancient times when heroes and Gods, it is said, walked the earth – where they feasted, warred and wed? Well, who is to say, I've not had my day or left a wake in my passing? Who is to say what voice spoke when mad men hearkened to hear what they could from lifeless forms made of stone or wood? What did mystics hear in their ear when kings commanded them to divine their god's will only to have fleets lost at sea, or have their venture riddled with misfortune and finally have their life's blood spilt?"

I sat bolt upright, "What do you mean by that?" I waited for the whispered answer – none came and I was reminded that whenever I moved Wind had to find my ear all over again.

I lay back down to quietly begin telling Wind everything from where I was born, about my first dad, my step-dad, "the rage machine," how mom changed and that we did not get along and then about day I ran away. Wind asked for a good memory so I recounted a summer day. I was riding on my bike when ice cream wagon passed me nearly knocking me over. The mean ugly driver yelled at me. No one liked this "Good Humor" man. Right after the truck was stuck at a stoplight and I was forced to stop behind the back door popped open and I had a rare opportunity. I looked around. While the truck idled, I filled my bike's basket with as much ice cream as I could grab in the short time I had. I brought the stuff back only to give it away to all the neighbor kids. It was great. Later, I had to make up a lie saying I found a twenty-dollar bill to buy the ice cream. My parents laughed and laughed. That was when everything was neat and everyone was happy.

After I fell asleep, Joey and I went out. Before we went anywhere, I looked down on me. It was like looking in a mirror, except my eyes were closed; you can't see in a mirror when you do that. I checked the area around – nothing was wrong. I looked around for Wind but there was nothing to see. Then we went out and up to the stars; we went around a couple of them. We rode back down along gravity's gradient. It was like riding a long, long, long slide. I liked the ride, though Joey watched the stars as we went. He thought about them a lot. Joey always wants always to go to other places especially all the old ones. I do not like them much; they are not any kind of fun mostly. He reads the books and things on walls; I do not. I got him to agree to trade off I chose a place or he does, one for one.

5/7/83

Dear Joey,

It is funny. I've not dreamt in the last two days. Joey says I do not want to remember what I dreamt with him. I told him he should tell me although he will not. I bet him he could not because I didn't dream. Wind has not been around either. I am ok though. I've food. I walk many miles each day. I sleep like a dead rock. Most of the country around here is hilly pasture with not much water so I've to take it easy with my canteen.

Yesterday, I talked to a man on horseback. I had not been on a trail. He came up on me without warning as I took a short cut through a fenced hilly pasture where I had seen a couple of big black cows. I was scared, however his talk was friendly. He looked a lot like a cowboy, boots, and hat with a sweatband, rough jeans and vest. He even made lunch for me in a real ranch house. He fixed beans with bacon poured over fried bread as well as hamburger meat in a soup of tomato sauce with noodles. We had jam and butter on bread and some sliced cold apples for desert. I did not know food could taste this good. He let me eat all I wanted. He told stories. I wanted to see the real cowboy stuff he said he would show me after he came back from a quick errand. He told me to "stay and make yourself real comfortable." He said he'd show me his grandpa's six-shooter, an old tractor as well as an ice cream maker, which he still used. It was going to be cool. He said he would be "back in a couple of a few minutes" those are the exact words and the way he said it. I was careful; when he went out, I went to the wind got very still. "Wind," I whispered.

It was there as if it had never left, "There you are, you've gone quite far. I guess you know that it is time to go. That man is going to phone. He knows you are too young to be out this far and alone. The police will come to take you away, pack up, get your food, and take the things you can. Do not stay. He's a good man, this is his farm; he wishes you no harm."

I put cereal, dried food packs and some canned meats in my pack. I left him a pile of change; it was heavy anyway. I silently made my way out the door. Once outside I began to jog quickly. I was half way to the back gate when I heard him yell after me. I booked on out of there. He was after me, and man he was fast. I heard his footfalls gaining quickly. I knew I wouldn't be able to outrun him – even if I hadn't had a pack on. I yelled hopelessly hoping. Then a whoosh Wind swept in behind me; I heard him yelp in pain. I kept going for hills without looking back. When I got pretty far up, well into some trees, I felt safe enough to turn and take a look back. I crouched down watching as I caught my breath.

I saw a police car pull up. Then the cowboy, who had been sitting on a fence, carefully got down and limped badly as he went over to talk to one of the officers. The two officers then helped the injured man toward the house. Before they went inside, the cowboy pointed up toward the hills, so exactly at me, that I ducked down – silly though it was. I thanked Wind. At first, there was nothing to indicate it had heard me.

It said, "Thank you, this was fun to do. His talk seemed friendly you say yet he goes to check in straight away. He wants to bring the police; he gives them a call but that's not all. Even nice people wanting to do right think it is dangerous for you to be out night after night. Beware that when you speak about who you are and such, very little may be far too much."

The cowboy had made me talk, well, sort of. I wanted to brag a bit about making my own way well enough. I wanted to talk about something in my life without being fearful.

I left the area walking south, that's what the Wind said. In the afternoon, I crossed a freeway near Pleasanton but I didn't need anything so I kept going and slept that night in the hills. I whistled with the wind; it is lots of fun!

When I asked Wind what it was made of it said, "I am that I am as you are, aware is aware is aware, no matter that I am simply air – but there's more, it's true, for you, I work through the air, which is all I can say if speaking fair."

5/8/83, Amid the Stars, then Sunol

Dear Joey,

We went to the stars last night. Some of them were so weird. There was one with six other stars around it; each of them had planets as well. There was no life on any of them. I am still amazed at how stars are all different colors when you look at them right.

We did look for planets like our own. We could not find any. We will still go out to look. I am certain there are some; Joey says there is not. He says every time I read a comic book I come up with stupid ideas.

I've plenty of food as well as money. When I took time to repack, I counted it all out to see what was what. Before I got on my way, I asked Wind why people were after me as if I'd done something bad. Wind puffed in my face a bit stiffly, this means to stop and listen. When nothing came, that meant to wait where I was. We have some tricks worked out.

I sat down. After a while, I began to read a cowboy book I had taken from the ranch out of curiosity. It was all about how Indians lived before the Europeans came to the Americas. Joey read along, of course, and memorized everything. The Indians ate all sorts of things, which grow around, leaves, roots, flowers, nuts and roots, even some water plants. The book had pictures and plant maps showing where certain plants lived, what they look like and when they are ready. I found I was sitting near wild lettuce. I tried it. It was ok. Joey said it would taste better if I washed it.

From above I heard a rustling of paper. I looked up. There was a whole collection of newspaper whirling about in a tight cloud. I stared. This was a new trick for Wind; it tried to say something, but I was not still enough to hear it. When the cloud of churning sheets finally landed, I gathered them up, oh and there was a good amount of paper money too.

"Read what you need," said Wind after I was still.

My mom was in a hospital being taken care of. My step-dad was in tough trouble. He had beaten her nearly to death and, since I was nowhere to be found, they believed I had run away because he had beaten me badly as well, which is all true. There was speculation that I might be dead, despite what both of them said. They had dogs searching for me. Since the house had also been robbed, a few thought someone else was involved. Overall, it looked as though stupid head old Vince would be in a heap of trouble unless or until I came back. Later papers reported I was object of a search in nearby parks. It was nice they were looking in all the wrong places. The retired ranger, the very cowboy I had talked with, had his picture in the paper. He said he had seen a child that looked like me, and Vince was quoted as saying he thought it impossible for me to anywhere near that far.

However, as long as I was out, Vince would have trouble. We, Joey and I, liked the thought. Then, suddenly, I burst into sobbing fell into what I called "blind crying." I didn't want mom thinking I was dead. However, after I stopped, I wondered if maybe my being out on my own and having them think I was dead was worth it – if she decided to leave Vince that is. Besides, I could always go back when she was home and not with him. In addition, the longer she stayed in a hospital, the less he could hurt her, in fact he couldn't hurt her at all. She would get good food and could not get drunk.

5/9/83

Dear Joey,

Today's papers say I could be a determined runaway. Some think I escaped well-planned searches. Most think I am dead. I've my picture in the paper. Joey says I am a sensation; he thinks coverage will last for a while. I hope it does not go on forever. I want to be old news. I do not think things will ever be ok. From what I read the cowboy did not know I was the runaway – at least at first. Papers say I stole stuff. That's another reason the police are involved. Some church groups or charities are concerned too. They are organizing volunteers to help search. I do not know the way to go now; Joey says I do not have to do anything. Wind says there is no hurry and not to worry. Well, I've my tent, sleeping bag, money and food – I guess I am ok.

I do not like staying in one place. I tried to talk them into going south but, finally, I just began walking. I kept to the hills and wound up near to the San Antonio Reservoir. There were few people around. I made camp well inside a group of trees. The walking was good. I felt better. Wind brought newspapers; and there was a bunch of paper money mixed in – it was great. I read the papers it was thought that if I wasn't dead I was hiding. If I was hiding, Vince must have been pretty bad. Also, if I had taken to stealing, I was not only in danger but could become dangerous. The bad news was it did not look like I was being ignored. Still, I was glad Vince would stay in trouble as long as I stayed away. If I could keep hidden, they would think I was dead. They had no proof I was alive; I mean really, so eventually they might treat Vince as a murderer. To me, the bottom line was he could not hurt mom anymore. All I've to do is wait. I sure wish I could grow in a hurry.

I found some onions growing in a field and nearby more wild lettuce and spinach. A walnut tree is not too far away. I will stay a couple of days; there is lots of food around. Wind brings stuff in too – it even brought a pizza in a box while it was still warm!

5/10/83

Dear Joey,

Today I went into Sunol. On the way, I stopped to see the water temple. It was beautiful. It made me think of ancient Greece. It is a neat little round building with columns. I took a nap and had a daydream. In it I saw women strolling in colorful dresses, the long ornate old-fashioned kind I've seen in historical paintings. The men wore straw hats; they strolled around on a big lawn area. A band was playing in what they called a gazebo. There were lots of kids. They were all playing near the tables where food was set out. Some were playing with hula-hoops though not in the right away. They rolled them on the ground, running along side, hitting them with a stick to keep them rolling. Others were having a three-legged race or playing baseball. It was a bright, clear summer day.

I went with some of the boys down to a creek where we caught frogs. We put a couple of them in a picnic basket. They scared the living daylights out of a woman when she peeked inside. I won some change from the kids when we shot for odds and evens. Joey could easily sneak a peek and tell me what to show in order to win.

I woke up it was the real day and time, except I still had a pocket full of change from a long time ago.

I went into Sunol to get some ice cream and look around. I sort of worried if anyone would recognize me but no one did. I got a paper. I had to go to a back section to find my story. There was no picture. Vince was on trial for criminal abuse. There was no word about mom. I recalled gangster movies where they talked about laying low until the heat blows over and so this is what I had to do.

Sunol is a small place. A church was showing a movie. I paid to see it; they had real good homemade popcorn and natural root beer; it was super great. I did my laundry. No one noticed me. I went back to camp with canned beans, hotdogs, bread, bananas, oranges and tea; food costs a lot. I slept well enough.

5/11/83

Dear Joey,

I went back into town to walk around. I found the library. I read books about the stars, history, and dreams. I did not understand the books on dreams though; they certainly did not agree with our experience. Anyway, the librarian spent a lot of time with me; she said I was a quick learner or, "bright as a dime." I thought mom, as she was in the good old days, would have liked her. When she asked if I was new in town, I told her I was staying for a week or so with some friends of my family while my dad traveled to Europe on business. Luckily, she did not ask more, though I thought she wanted to.

It was odd though, talking to her at first, I kept wondering if she recognized me or if there was some other reason for her being extra nice. For a time I believed she was simply seeing me for whom I was, individually; I mean as a person so, it was possible there was something like a friendship developing. Then too, since I was curious, always wanting to learn, we had a common interest. I stayed on just outside of town.

I will go to the library tomorrow, maybe see a movie. I still have a lot of money. I get more every time Wind brings me the papers. I had thought about getting some job but maybe I will never need one. I am doing ok right now. I know I cannot go back home yet, that's clear from the papers.

At my camp, I made a soup with greens with some wild potatoes. I seasoned it with spices – my own mix. I like to cook;

it is fun and easy. I wish I had an icebox – though I could not very well keep one of those.

I do not feel bad much. I don't know where I want to go or what I want to do when I get there. We go around to lots of places in dreams, Wind tells me stories before I go to sleep; the weather is nice.

I asked Wind what holds me back or makes me unhappy. I heard, in the stillness, "What holds you back? You have no track, so you cannot tack; no heading, it is true, you have nothing to do; it is like water your treading. So wait, be aware you'll want to do more than survive. You must do what you do. Keep to what is true, avoid strife – remember you are love made into life!"

5/14/83

Dear Joey,

I am on the move again. The last time I went into town, the librarian spent a lot time with me and I felt odd about it. I got a few books on modern history. I was looking for patterns. I kept quiet and didn't ask questions. Joey says she saw me take out my roll of money as I put it in order then back inside my wallet. After that, she watched me from a distance all the time. I think she heard me talking to you Joey. Joey you do not always watch to see if someone is looking when you ask me something. Why do you do that? She probably considered me a real nut basket.

She came over at one point, we started talking but soon she got to working in innocent seeming questions. First, they were only about where I went to school or things I liked to do with family. I had lies ready in an instant, Joey can sure cook them up, short order. I told her I was Jan Bentley – I cleverly used my real first name while the last name I got from a book I saw on a shelf behind her. Later, I laughed at having all the wrong and misleading answers for her inquiring mind.

I was alert. Just because the librarian is an older woman does not mean she is not clever or a possible threat. Her face is round though she is seemingly underweight. She talks funny as well. She has a cleft palate. I found out you are born with it. I felt for her. I know how kids can make fun of you. I learned she has been in the town for twenty years but had no connections.

She does not feel a part of it. She lives alone except for her cat. I think she likes me. Most people do not use the library often. Those that do, don't talk with her much about anything except business. While she talked, I had an imagination dream. I saw her crying, wanting to be held, soothed, cared for or loved. This made me miss my mom so much I cried full on right in front of her.

When she asked about my tears, I opened up telling her about everything, the true story. However, I changed the names, places, and some vital details. I told her I lost my real dad and, because of "Victor," my mom, well kind of. I told her about the happy times with my real dad, the picnics, singing, playing cards or telling stories after dinner. I sighed saying it was all a long seeming time ago so I hardly remembered most of it since that was before Joey, the bad times, and Victor. I didn't have to play up my dislike of Victor.

I told her my most secret story. One night, late, my mom's voice scared me awake. She and my real dad were arguing – not so much with each other as complaining. They stopped short when I walked in the kitchen. My dad turned to me and asked me if I'd like a brother or a sister. I felt very funny feelings in my stomach; it was so weird I did not know what to say. My mom swooped me up and asked me if I was happy with the house. I remember saying they were the "bestest parents I ever had." I felt so happy when they laughed. I was happy they were happy. I made my duck and pig noises, which always made them laugh. I sang a silly song and they laughed even harder. It was going to be all right. I wanted to keep them happy. I did my funny acts, the Gumby imitation and singing Tip Toe through the Tulips. I could not keep it up for long. I could not do it for them all by myself. When ran out of my acts, they soon stopped laughing. The silence got very thick and strong. I had failed.

My mom put me back to bed then they both went out of the room. Soon they were back at it again. Mom saying something about his being all worked up over getting a doctor's help for some kind of carriage. The word "problem" came up a lot. They said stuff about mind problems. They were talking over and interrupting each other. I could not stand it. They acted ugly. Both said you said this or that, or I did not mean that or this but something else or the other. Mom sounded very tired. After a while, she said she did not want to talk any more. She could not deal with it. He hollered out something, which she took as his agreement. He said part of the problem was they would never talk much less do anything about their feelings for each other, no matter how strongly felt, what they desperately wanted, or vitally needed. I finally came to understand what a miscarriage was by overhearing bits and pieces of talk. It had happened twice before I was born, once more since. So I understood what she meant when she said, "there wasn't going to be any damned next time to be different" and they both cried I was deeply shocked and horribly depressed for a long time.

Later, she came into my room, closed the door to sit with me while he was still talking, which made him cuss strongly and go outside. She soothed my brow, tucked me in and shushed me the few times I tried to speak. Later, I awoke slightly. I heard her still in the room, humming. I called out to her, "What was the fight all about?"

She said some things cause people to fall out of love and into despair. My birth had not been an easy one and they had begun their marriage with plans for several children. She said they were learning just how was hard it was to give up something they had both dreamt of and cherished. Tears brimmed at her lids. When one raced down it twinkled; and she looked aside, into the soft light she was terribly beautiful.

The librarian smiled; she liked that part of the story. I did not tell her the most important part how I began to hear a voice talk to me inside my head.

But because she was so touched, I added in the part about how I pretended to go to sleep for my mom, which is how I knew that, as dawn's breath sent lighter shades stealing into the room, she kissed me and left quietly. I went to sleep for real. I did not hear my dad come home. In the morning, although things were ok, they were never the same. The new way of things did not last for long. Dad died a few weeks later, in an accident. I will always wonder what it would have been like, really, if he had lived.

The librarian was sad for me.

I told her about a time I buried a kitten; it had followed me home, well that's what I told mom anyway. She let me keep it. A few days later, when I went to get my bike to go to school, I found it on the garage floor – limp and cold. I hid the creature in some bushes after quickly wrapping it in old newspaper. When I got back home, I buried it and said prayer words over it. I told my folks it must have run off.

There was another time when I made breakfast in bed for mom and dad on their anniversary; soon it became a tradition in our family on birthdays, of course such a things went out the window as soon as the bad times began.

I told her about a time I cried about not having a Christmas tree on as it got close to the first Christmas after my dad died. I was afraid we couldn't afford it since mom had always been talking about a shortage of money and then too, everything was different.

I cried again when I told her about a time when mom lit birthday candles in front of me because I couldn't help recalling the happy days, in the old house, when the candles from birthday cakes would always reflect off the blue and white tile backsplash behind the sink. I liked being able to see the cake before it was brought through the doorway.

I did not care if she saw all those memories fall out; or if I cried a little bit from time to time as I kept on talking until I felt sort of empty, maybe lighter and a little bit good.

I guess she had to ask questions after that, but, even so, if the librarian had not asked questions, I'd have left. I had been in one place to long. After I decided to leave, I bought a nice card, put it in a small box with a large, beautiful arrangement of cut wildflowers. I wrote in my best letters about how I had to leave with my parents. I told her she was a good person; I liked her and thanked her for helping me learn how to use a library. I told her she reminded me of my favorite aunt and, yes Joey, I know I do not have an aunt so shut up as if I do not know. I told her because I thought she would feel good. She needed that.

I put the box on the top step to the library with her name written on it very early in the morning. I was going to hide nearby so I could see her pick it up however I decided not to. The giving was enough. As I walked out of town, I imagined the different ways she'd react.

I was a few miles into the countryside when a police car passed me by going the other way; I pretended to "act normal." When it pulled over to stop, I kept walking nonchalantly. I went up the driveway of what looked to be an empty home and through its backyard gate; it was a real gamble. As soon as I was out of sight, I jumped the yard's fence to hide and then took off like a shot. I do not take chances. I waited for a while before sneaking off into an orchard and crossed through a vineyard. I got to a cross roads where there was only the one gas station. I bought a map and changed clothes. I headed for the Calaveras Reservoir, that's where they have the famous frog-jumping contest, though I couldn't remember when they did that.

5/15/83

Dear Joey,

Do not be jealous of Wind, look how much it helps us out. Just go along with it over the hills and through the pastures. I am happy walking freely; I know you like it too.

I camped near the reservoir while managing to stay out of sight. Wind said it would watch over and warn until dawn. I asked it if it ever slept.

"Sleep? Not a peep. How can I close my great, deep blue eye? I am I. I've always been so – know to know is my credo, so, sleep, yes, make not a peep. God bless you and keep. I'll watch over you from now until the dawn lights upon your brow."

I felt good. I could swim all I wanted. I like to swim. At home, we would only go to a local park where they had a small wading pool for the kids. I could barely float in it. You could see the adults swimming in the creek a few yards away. That was not for kids, even to wade in. They would never let me try. This was something else altogether. Where I was however, I could swim as far out as I wanted to and the wind would blow me back toward shore.

I've lots of food. I am not worried about money either. Although I made a practice of keeping Vince out of my mind, I did have a daydream about him. You saw it Joey, the one where he and mom get back together. I never though she would do it – yet she did. So I wasn't surprised when the next time Wind brought the paper we saw it, right? The picture showed them happily celebrating at a reunion. They both want me back. They looked happy enough. I do not know if I want to go back, yet.

5/17/83, The Gangly Man

Dear Joey,

The papers Wind brought this morning's papers, which say my parents are offering a reward for information. It says a librarian contacted them after she brought my note to the police. Of course, I they figured it was real by handwriting analysis.

Analysis is my newfound word for today. Bad news is now they are sure I am alive.

They want me back. If they are happy, I do not have to go. I can go back anytime I want. I am going to move again. I am not far from where I was last seen. The heat is on, as "Bugsy" Moran would say.

One of the campers told me about Big Basin State Park. I think I will go there. Milpitas was the first city I came to when I left the hills. I bought some maps of intercity buses. I did not want to walk around the city at night. However, not having a refuge, or hiding place, I walked down Warm Springs Boulevard right into San Jose.

It was night by the time I got to a place I could get a bus. I waited for a long while; it was cold too so I went into a 24 Hour DoNutz. I need to stay there for a while so I told the man behind the counter I was on my way to my parents and was waiting for a bus. He did not seem to care about anything. He hardly spoke. I had milk with doughnuts, making sure I only showed change when I paid. I got worried when a police car pulled up. I was sitting in the back though. By the time they came in, I was holding up a newspaper. I kept behind it pretending to read. I had an adult like hat on – I was covered. They talked forever. I worried that the bus would show up while they were there and I'd have to risk walking past them and did not feel safe trying to leave. After they left, and the counter man went to the back, I lifted a few milks and some napkins before walking out; I did not want him to remember me or risk him seeing through my lie. I walked the bus route and found out the bus I had hoped to catch was only a daytime line. The connecting point between it and the one I wanted to transfer to was some miles off. I shrugged and hunched into the cold breeze and kept on walking. It was in the middle of the night. I had on dark clothes and I worked my way through the streets of downtown San Jose. Everything was fine until, on a narrow back alley, Wind came from above with such force I knew I should duck down, down, hide fast. Wind blew some papers and heavier trash over me so I was "under cover" yet at the scene.

In a minute, a police car slowly drove through the alley with its spotlight moving all around and tires crunching through trash on the gritty ground. I knew they were not looking for me. Then it stopped, not far off, and its doors opened. Two officers slowly got out, with care then focused their flashlights on a loading dock of some older building with corrugated iron walls. I crouched tight. When, close on by me, a garbage can clattered, they played their lights all around my location as they jogged over searching. Next, and not far off, another officer yelled, and, somewhere in that direction someone else yelled back before there was an exchange of gunfire. The officers near me ran off in that direction. Moments later I heard a garbage can fall over and some clattering noise and someone else came running along. This one-stepped on my back before clambering over the chain link fence. I heard heavy breathing, a rustling sound, and then nothing. A couple of sirens could be heard approaching the area now and, in the farther distance, there was another burst of shots. It wasn't long before two other officers ran through the alley and a little while later the first two came back bringing a handcuffed man along. They stopped to catch their breath and questioned him as they roughly searched him. They hit him a few times when he would not tell who or where his friend was or where that friend might go. In my mind, Joey and I argued over whether or not he knew but I didn't care.

For a while, the guy sat in the police car as one officer called in and the other walked about shining his light to the ground looking for clues. Joey and I got scared. It seemed like forever, when, for a while, he stood right above me, his boot toe a few feet from my nose. My old coat fit in with the pile of anonymous trash, anonymous is my new four-syllable word for today by the way. Joey says he is always anonymous. It was so funny I almost giggled. All the while, I crouched there, the whole time, right under my nose in fact, there was this trail of ants going by as calmly as ever. For a while, I tried to count how many went one way as well as the other. I kept loosing count; anyway, I'd say more than a thousand passed by. It helps if you count them by fives or tens. A garbled dispatch call came over their radio and they left in a hurry. I waited some time before I moved. I'd have waited even longer if my left leg had not fallen asleep before cramping up something fierce. I had to stand up.

My mind screaming in pain, I carefully looked around as I slowly got up. I stood still whispering for Wind to guide me. Fresh breezes picked up I hurried to follow them along the alley. I hadn't gone far when I heard footsteps from behind. Wind stilled. I stopped and turned to look. This tall, gangly scruffy man stopped too. He had a long, drawn and bony face and a dirty forehead, which was surmounted by disheveled, dark curly hair. He was jittery. His face was pale and he seemed to be sweating even though it was fairly cool outside. He had some facial scabs, was speckled with a rash, and his clothes were rumpled and dirty.

"Hey kid, I wanta say you did good, real good. They never even looked at you except as trash, hey ... don't back off – no need. I'm cool." I backed off even more as he said that.

"What do you want with following me?"

"I'm not following you, you're going my way. Say, how old are you to be out here like this anyway?"

"It sure looks like following to me!" I said backing up my tone trying to act tough. He kept on inching closer. It was as if he thought by keeping eye contact, he could move in on me without notice. I got worried. I did not think I could outrun him unless I had starting distance. Why did I talk to him at all? I don't know even now. He looked so frail, maybe ill. I felt he wanted to help me, I guess.

"You were good, you let me jump on you and froze like a pro while they were around, even when they stood right over you. Even during all that shooting you stayed calm, acting just like garbage is supposed to act, I admire that."

"What do you expect me to do, stand up and say, " 'Would you all please stop this I'm scared' or something? I mean I've reasons for doing what I do, believe me."

"I'll bet you do, little brother, I'll bet you do." He was moving forward again gesturing easily with his hands as he chatted me up.

"Hey," I said, "Are you the other guy they were looking for?" The loud barking tone of the question, no doubt, checked his movement but only for a moment. He stopped to stretch, his arms reaching upwards as he twisted his torso to look around. He said, as if in confidence, "Nah, the only crime I done is not having a place to live or any kind of work. Look at me, who'd hire me?"

"Why did you hide?" I said checking him again, this time with more volume of voice hoping someone would hear, I'd welcome the police at this point; I clenched my fists.

"Listen, little brother, those bully boys were looking for someone to bust up. I saw the lights coming; I had to hide. I saw them before you did. I watched you walk by me. I was right to hide; we were both right. I hid as well as you did, better. I hid first, see?" He laughed a bit and looked at ease. I wondered if maybe, maybe I could be at ease too. I needed someone to trust. I'd like to find out how he made it. He lived in a city without a place to live. I'd like to know how he did it, for sure.

"I know you need a place to stay. Right? Probably got a drunken dad, got sick of being beat on, so you broke into the cookie jar, took the house money and ran away. Well I can help you out." How could he read me so well? I stood there as he took another step toward me. I couldn't figure a move; I got ready to strike. His eyes took all of me in as he moved without a sound, talking in a whisper, I whispered to follow his example.

"Do you live around here?"

"Sure not too far at all."

"Where?"

"Over near Eastridge Mall there is an overgrown back lot next to a highway. A few of us got a camp."

"Where is that?"

"It's a bit of a way, little buddy. You can make it, sure." With that, he walked past me. I was surprised. I began to follow. We walked in silence. I gradually decided on a safe distance to maintain, I didn't want to get too close. His calm voice and attitude was quite out of step with his nervousness or apprehensive cat-like ways. We talked a very little. Right in the middle of something he was muttering, to himself, I guess, I saw a daydream. In it I was lying down upon the broken pavement of this very alley, out cold, bleeding from my mouth. There was a lot of blood flowing from the back of my head making a dark pillow sized pool. He was going through my pack desperately furtive. I was watching this from above as if in a dream.

I noticed the quiet all around me, no Wind, nothing. I was watched his feet as I walked behind him but stopped still as I heard a smooth metal click. He spun quickly around. His arm flashed out and the swishing sound of a broad wicked blade was close. Even though I had anticipated the move and had ducked down, I wasn't fast enough to move off so when he whipped his arm back, he hit me hard with butt end of his knife and I sprawled flat on my back. I desperately scuttled backwards but the ground was slick; my shoes were slipping. As he advanced in a crouch brandishing the blade he made kind of gross, gargle of a giggle while tossing the glittering blade from hand to hand. When he lunged in I kicked at it and he lost his grip on the wicked weapon. Distracted, as he fumbled, I flipped around and ran off. Something hit me in the head so hard I blinked all the way out. I was down on all fours feeling woozy, sick dizzy when I could see again.

There was a rushing sound. Wind bowled him over then swept him away from me. When it cut off, he stood up, looked around in typically weasel-like, Vince-like, way before fixing on me. He took a couple of steps before whirling air surrounded him. He looked all around and up; he was inside his own private tornado. I stood up as he angrily jumped up and down, hollering, acting all frenzy-crazy as my head cleared. I gathered my stuff. I picked up his knife after Wind had pinned him against a filthy brick wall of a building. I was amazed at how quietly it acted. The man was pinned to the wall yet there was no sound above that of a rushing breeze moving through treetops. He couldn't talk; too much air was rushing around him. I told Wind to let him go. He fell down in a heap, unconscious.

"I did not know he would be violent, by his scent he was in pain that was plain. I did not know what to do when he hurt you. When I saw you fall, I forced him away that's all. I kept him at bay until you were ok. When you set let go; I did so. He is ok. He will sleep on well through the day."

I took the man's pulse. Joey said it was strong enough, regular, and the color was coming back into his face and hands. I searched his pockets and jacket. I found about 500 dollars along some white powder in little plastic bags – drugs of some kind. I sprinkled the powder on his lips as well as on the ground around him. I then took his leather jacket, fancy shoes, belt and watch in order to pawn them. Soon after I used a pay phone, called the police, and finked him out big time for the shooting and, putting words in his mouth I did my best to frame him for it. I said he had over dosed on drugs. I told them where he was. Joey had told me where one of the guns were. I put it in his pocket, emptied of bullets of course, before I left. I got lots more money after I ran his credit cards, rummaged his apartment then cashed a few checks. We were doing a good job of "helping him out."

5/18/83

Dear Joey,

I walked around town today. I could take care of myself. I remembered dreaming of that guy from a few days past.

I figured out a good one, I called a motel, put a cloth over the phone while I talked in a deep voice. I spoke like a parent; all I had to do was repeat what Joey said. It worked; they thought my "child" was going to be showing up there. I paid with one of that guy's credit cards. I told them the kid was 18 but didn't look it. They believed me since their place was not far from Great America. I took a bus there to the park.

I bought soda, hot dogs before going on a bunch of real fun rides. Wind helped push a sailboat I was in; we went fast. I asked Wind to knock over some targets so a kid in a wheelchair could win a prize. He was very happy. I felt good I laughed myself silly off and on the whole time I was there.

When I strolled into the motel with trinkets and souvenirs, the motel people did not ask much of anything at all. I didn't need another story but I had a good few ready, believe you me. I've lots of money. They called me "mature." They just believed I was 18. I can stay here for some good while.

5/19/83

Dear Joey,

When I went to Great America again someone told me about the Frog Jumping contest was going to happen in a few days. I decided to rest up, go to Great America one more time before going to check it out. I talked with Wind after I heard on the news about a drought in a far part of the world. I asked if it could do something about to help.

"You'd guess I'd say yes. Yes?"

"You can, you can do everything; you saved my life."

"You have more to know, you know. I cannot tell you why or why not; sometimes I am in a spot. I will try to let you see how what will be will be. True it is, I do gift the land with water, the cool rains fall, yet does a father love his daughter if he always gives her everything, anytime at all no matter how big or small?"

"I don't understand Wind, why do bad things go on."

"You must grow. To grow you must rest; this is just and best. I must go while you must sleep, please pray for those for whom you'd weep."

5/21/83

Dear Joey,

Today when I went to Great America, I found I had left most of my money at the motel. If the window was open, Wind could have gotten it for me, even though it might have left the

room as if a cyclone had hit it. I got into the park as I had
enough money for that in my pocket. Still, I was disappointed;
I'd not have enough for all the rides. I did not want to go back.
I'd not have enough time to get on all the rides I planned to. It
was hot. I turned around to walk back toward the gate when
Wind guided me behind a partially completed building.
"Open your coat so you can float."
"What?"
"Do it for me; you'll see."
I opened up my coat but kept each hand gripped to the
corner where the zipper ends met the bottom seams. Wind swept
up into it, ballooning it big. I went up quickly. I was scared you
bet – yet I was flying! Well, sort of. Wind put me down near my
motel where no one would see. I went right in, got my money
then came right back out. Wind dropped me back inside the park
– Wind said it was ok, as I had already paid. It was the best ride
ever. After that I wasn't scared of any ride in the park.
I stood real still, asked, "Why didn't you do when I was
in trouble before in San Jose?"
Wind replied, "This is as new to me as it is to you; you
will note you have a big, strong coat." I had a great time the
whole day.
The next day I woke up late, took a taxi to the museum
Joey had read about. Joey wanted me to see it. Joey told me all
the stories about the paintings and statues. I had a hot dog with
everything on it, a real soda fountain soda then an ice cream. We
spent the whole day there walking all over. I was tired when we
came back; I guess we will go tomorrow.

5/22/83

Dear Joey,

After something of a nightmare involving some eerie
men with dark glasses I decided to leave off, very early, about 3
a.m. The staff was friendly yet I got a feeling I should book on
out, as a couple of them seemed to be getting friendlier, very
engaging, and seemed to be getting curious about me, my folks,
as they tried to be conversational about where I came from. I
wanted to stay in a nice, clean place for a while but their
friendliness made me anxious. Joey argued with me saying he

hadn't noticed anything, however, as I put it, "That's maybe the whole point, wingnut!"

The intercity bus did not get me to Calaveras. I made a mistake by getting on the wrong bus. I looked at maps as it went along before deciding to get off near Alum Rock Park. At least I was within hiking or hitching distance. I took off into the hills. I had a good ways to go that's why I took as straight a course as geography or private property allowed. I was confident I could get there; I mean to say it was still early in the morning.

I was in luck. I followed a road, which took me in the right direction, which had me chance upon a Christian youth outreach group forming up at a high school. I was able to get ride with several busloads of kids. They were going to the contest – all I had to do was pay ten dollars for the day trip, no questions no ID required, it was super cool.

I had a lot of plain simple fun with them. I even bet and lost. I could have won though. I had Wind help this one guy. I do not know why we wanted to; we just did. It was easy for Wind to help the guy's frog set a record. I felt great; later I found out people bet on the contest. I could have won a bundle, oh well.

I stayed with those kids mostly. It was good – oh some tried to talk to me about the Bible while few of the girls were cute and friendly, I guess, though when they went on and on about relationships with God, it was pretty scary stuff, no kidding! I mean they had never seen the olden days and the elder gods as I had. When it was time for them to leave I left with the same group I came with. When I got back to the to the school, I got a ride to Saratoga after I played up some interest. They took me along to some kind of revival at a campground in a public park. I knew enough of their "language" to be accepted. Once there, in the confusion, I ducked to get on my way, again heading for the hills. From them I got a nice compass, mess kit, some handy gear, food as well as a good bit of money. I could have taken a car too. I have to say I thought about it although I had to agree with Joey; it was too risky. I put all the old cooking stuff and supplies I had taken from home into a Goodwill box after I had washed them and wrapped them up inside a clean paper bag.

5/24/83

Dear Joey,

I made it into the hills then capped off the day by finding a real nice little spot not too far from the highway. I ate cereal, got in my sleeping bag then fell asleep as I prayed. The sky was beautiful; I loved all the stars. I went to sleep.

We went to a city under water. We played hide and seek among statues. Wind could not get in at all. Joey found a ring. It was exquisitely beautiful. He gave it to me.

I dreamt dogs were approaching where I slept. The dogs were lean, mean faced, angry, and, what's more, they ran as a pack. There were humans with them. I caught a whiff cigarette smoke and sweat, all men. Wind, seeing this, swept them far away.

I've always been afraid of dogs. A long time ago, in the good old days, some of us were playing hide-and-seek over where some new houses were being built. Somehow, we wound up chasing each other into the back yard of a newly finished house. Its yard had not been planted; and was marked out only with fence posts. I was trying to escape someone and managed to hide behind a trashcan. Figuring I was safe I got up and was sneaking along when, out of nowhere, a real big dog, maybe a St. Bernard or something, came out charging, growling and barking. I ran like a bat out of hell for my very life! I clawed and scrambled my way up a tree before and jumped over a fence into another yard. Take that for scary, I wished Wind had been with me back then, boy oh boy do I!

The weirdest thing was that I still had I the weird old ring! When I asked Joey how could a dream have real things in it – he said a dumb thing about how different people have different kinds of dreams. He added everything is a dream in someone's eyes sometime or another. I blinked in puzzlement then we argued for a long time. He was right about one thing – the ring is here. It sure enough is the most beautiful, ever. Wind said it was very old and could bring trouble. I thought that was because people would want it as soon as they saw it.

After I ate breakfast, Joey said I should use one of my spare leather bootlaces to hang it a round my neck in order to keep it under my shirt, out of sight, and not likely to be lost. I wore it over my heart. Soon, it felt as if it was magnifying the sunlight or the heat of the day; it was quite warm. Joey said it was doing that and much more. He said the inscriptions on the ring, it was covered with them, had terms for force or energy, movement, growth, and change. This was the literal translation. However, he did not know what they all actually meant together. I felt happy just holding it. For once Joey did something nice for me and me alone.

5/29/83, Sick, Captured, and an Escape

Dear Joey,

I walked all today. It was simple enough to get into the parkland up in the hills. I hope to stay for some time. There are way less people and I bet it'll be easier to stay hidden. Joey, I hope you are right about the newspapers you read. If there are people, men mostly, living in the hills, I can learn to live such a like way as they do too.

On my way through the hills, I found a spring. I thought it could be a great spot to rest for a few days. I had lunch. The spring was fed by seasonal run off. Not long after some few cows meandered by then even more came. I did not care. I got on my way as soon as I finished eating. I filled my canteen. I hoped to be over the next set of ridges by late afternoon. I was going to make an entry by the park's north side. I did not want to bother using a regular entrance. I strained to make it.

I started feeling tired then had a fit of shivers. The water must have been bad. I took out my salt; mixed a lot of it in a cup of water, tossed it back, in a moment, I was throwing up all over the place. I ate the sprouts, which hadn't finished sprouting yet, and drank their tinged water. I felt a bit better. I walked on not knowing what to do – fearing I'd have to see a doctor. I did not want to lay up only to be asked all the inevitable questions while in a place I couldn't easily escape from. I chewed the bitter root of a plant Joey pointed out. I felt ok, for a while although I could not find any more and got worse again. Now I wanted to find a doctor.

I was hurting bad when I came within sight of some buildings. I started to get cramps in my stomach; I had the shivers. I had a story worked out though as soon as a ranger caught sight of me, he didn't ask any questions but got me to the camp doctor. I was switching from cold chills to hot then back again. As he covered me in a warmed blanket, he asked medical questions, intently at first. He did not seem worried when I told him about the spring water. He was stern and quiet. He let me stay on a nice cot in a small room, gave me some warm, clear broth with a couple of pills. My stomach felt much, much better then I was out like a light.

I woke up next day feeling all achy, weak, and very sluggish. Overall, I felt worse except not my stomach. I was glad they were taking care of me without asking questions. Even while wondered about that, I was glad to be warm, comfortable, and getting well.

The door to my little room was open. I could hear the activities of the office going on. I listened to them answer phones, talk over the radio to other rangers or deal with visitors to the park. I was by a window. When no one was looking, I opened it to talk with Wind. Wind told me all about the park. I was excited, eager to get well and rove around in it. I was not going to do anything until I was well; I promised Wind. I pretended to sleep while they went through my pack. I wondered why. It did not matter to me, my money was safely away and I had no ID. Escape from this place would be as easy as making up a story before walking away.

I was feeling better by the hour. I began to fear it was only a matter of time before I'd have some kind of trouble. I told them I was from Saratoga and wove my few real lies with some half-truths. We knew maps, Joey and I. We believed our story sounded good. I overheard them calling the local sheriff though it seemed difficult to get through to the right person. Even if they got through, a search for a missing person with my pretend name would turn up no matches. I acted as if I trusted them. I thought if I could work this for or maybe two or more I'd be good to go. However I was determined to get away clean, by that I mean without using Wind or leaving any kind of trail.

That night, however, a group of adults came in. They told me they were convinced of my real identity. They moved me to another room where someone watched me. They said my parents were darned worried about me. I did not know if such a thing was true – if it was it could be good or bad news.

When I asked if I could talk to them, they said they had tried to reach them but, according to a neighbor, they had gone on a trip. I was suspicious and figured it to be a lie.

If Vince and mom went away together, it could mean they were getting along, maybe doing well with money. Maybe he let mom work more or maybe he finally got a long-term construction job. Maybe they are talking more than drinking – which would be nice.

I gave up pretending to be sicker than I was.

I was sure I could get away, if it came to it. I wanted to do it all on my own. I got worried when I heard them say they'd keep me until someone came for me. I didn't like that.

As the day went on, everyone became concerned with spreading forest fires. One fire threatened the roadway leading into the park, which could isolate this compound. Another, not a dozen miles off was closing. Some worried the second fire would make it to the center. In a short time, the office became the fire fighting operations center and terribly busy. My escape plot depended on the chaos but the fire, being in several places, made it hard to avoid being seen no matter which way I went. There were too many people that could recognize me. I got up, walked to my pack, took out my notebook, and began to write. I had some catch up to do.

"So you like to play sleep!" I jumped as if jazzed with a shock stick. The mean nurse, I called "big nurse" after the one in Cuckoo's Nest, who been taking care of me, was right behind me. Fearing the worst, I slapped my book shut. I was not scared of her however. As I stood up, she glared down at me. "What?" I asked.

"Don't play innocent with me, you were out as far as I could tell with no likelihood of coming out of it anytime soon. I took your vitals. Now I come in to check you and find you looking as good as ever! Do you know we have people who are dangerously sick out there? We don't have time for games." Her face was vexed with righteous anger. I understood it perfectly. I did not think she would bat me upside the head. Still, the situation with the fire and the incoming needy had her working hard. I was embarrassed at what I had done; I apologized sincerely. I told her I had been told to stay where I was, tentatively adding a measure of the truth, "I have to get well, I can sleep my own way and it helps me heal."

"Well, I don't believe you." she snapped.

"I am sorry, besides, I had to know if you are going to send me home. If you were I had figure a way out of here; I want to escape from my parents – that's all – it has nothing to do with you."

Waving off the comment, she dismissively said, "Well, you won't be going anywhere soon, even the fire roads are out. You'll be handed over to a couple of rangers or the police if possible. We can't have someone like you taking up space like this no matter what else happens. I won't have it. So, for now, you'll just have to stay put, final! I'll be back in a minute."

In a moment later she unlocked the door and had me follow her to an office area where several persons were busied answering phones. "The rangers will come soon, you stay put you hear me?" she said sternly before telling the others I was the Long Runaway, my newspaper nickname, and had to be kept "inside, in sight, and out of trouble."

I was already thinking, what with the confusion and the way people all around kept coming and going, I could, eventually, walk out just as plain as you please without being missed. As if she read my mind, the nurse turned back around, looked at me hard as she called out to a man named Jess. A tall well-built, athletic man in a ranger's uniform stood up and walked over. "What you want, El," he said as gave me a look out of curiosity and listened to her.

"Take care of our little fugitive, he's ok now. Watch out though; he says he doesn't want to go home."

This man with a friendly face nodded at me and, surprisingly, when he smiled, I felt like smiling, so I did, honestly. "Is that so? Well, I'll watch him real good, El, no problem." He reached his hand out to me. Although I felt I had no choice in the matter, I felt glad enough to do shake his. I was still betting it was better to appear willing in order to work out an escape later when the opportunity came.

I asked Jess if I could help to make up for the inconvenience I had caused, he said, "Nah, take it easy, have a chair," indicating a folding chair across from where he was working. "She's sore you took a place she'd use for someone more in need. She definitely feels you lied and that doesn't sit well with her at all; I know." I told Jess, a bit angrily, I hadn't lied to her. I had been really, truly sick and was very sorry. He got that I hadn't planned to mess up anyone, least of all a nurse. I was ready with a new cover story to story to camouflage myself, I wanted to try it out on him, I had just started when the phone rang and he was intensely busy.

As it got busier, I took a seat some distance away. He pointed me out to everyone coming in however. I looked around. I couldn't leave by jumping through a locked window in plain sight nor did could running a gauntlet of manned desks, a tall counter, then the pair of heavy glass doors opening to the foyer, used for displays, before I could get to the second pair of heavy glass doors, the building's entrance.

I couldn't get in touch with Wind. I was closed off and besides it was noisy. Everyone was hollering into phones or radios. There were many folks with problems, one woman was having a baby, a boy was crying as a man put a cast put on his arm, others were sitting in spaces on the floor, sleeping, resting or waiting to be tended to.

It was getting worse by the minute as phones rang off the hook and hyper busy people came or went. I could see the place could not hope to cope. I began helping cleaning up spills, making coffee, handing things from one person to another, and making myself useful. These were good folks; their simple thanks was praise enough for me. Soon I was doing errands inside or took messages when no one else could get to the phone. They called me a "boy Friday" whatever that means.

When there was one of those illusory lulls in the action, I asked Jess if I could speak to him; he said, "Sure."

"Well, you have helped me out a lot, I guess. I want to help out the park and everyone here, can I?"

"You're doing pretty well right now; we're plenty thankful. You've been quite a hand ask anyone here."

"I mean I can help out with the fire…"

"Now you're too small for that, we have a couple thousand of men out there and they would be distracted watching out for you. Better you should stay here to help out." He had interrupted me just as Vince did. Why do they never listen? I bet anything Wind could stop this fire in a minute, sure.

"Listen, Jess, I've a friend who take care of this fire in no time at all, please listen, let me try. Ok?"

The phone started ringing. In a moment, Jess was handling three lines. He was the only one on the phones at that moment. Everyone else was outside working or other, tending the injured or caring for those traumatized. When the noise level went up a notch, I looked to see a whole set of kids come in with, I guess, their teacher along with a few parents. I began to plot: there was only one person manning the doorway, he was new on the shift; he didn't know me. I planned to use the other kids as distractions. I made the hard choice to sacrifice my pack but not my writing.

I worked my pack open, took out my book. I put on a heavy outer shirt, tucked it in tightly around my waist before putting the book down my shirtfront. I stuffed my pockets with what I could. I looked like I gained 20 pounds. Yet, all the while, I was in plain sight – no one noticed.

I looked over at Jess. The phone connection must have been bad. He was hollering to be heard as well as having difficulty hearing whomever it was as he tried to take notes. I sidled over toward the counter while keeping a roving eye on him and the others. Big Nurse was wrapping a little girl's head as she moaned. I moved along toward the coffee machine but couldn't figure a safe move when some bratty smart aleck kid wanted to know who I was – I couldn't have asked for more! I drew him, unknowingly, into my plans by bragging about my age and travels and he asked the teacher if I could help her hand out snacks and water. In this way, I worked my way toward the door. When I was close enough, I took my chance. With a few quick steps, I was opening the first set of doors but that darned nurse, she'd been around all the time, caught sight of me, yelled to a new guy who happened to be standing there and, because he lost a blink of time misunderstanding her intent and although he took a couple of long steps toward me once he did, I dodged him to get through the first set of doors. The second set was unguarded. I was out and picking up speed before that poor sucker could even get traction.

I shouldn't have glanced back to check on my pursuers so I didn't see a shallow puddle so I slipped, fell, and a nearby ranger, quickly sizing up both the situation and myself, was carrying me back tucked under his arm.

I struggled uselessly. He knew how to keep a hold while my extra bulk worked against me. He carried me back easily toward the doorway. I whistled for Wind; nothing came. Jess had followed the nurse out; he was stern looking; the nurse smug. I was literally being handed over when a blustery gust caught the nurse mid stride; she stumbled, fell and Jess, struggling to keep his feet, was unable to help her. The man holding me and I both went sprawling. A blast of wind pinned us all. I was too close to them for Wind to let me go while holding them each down.

I stilled while whistling. Wind stopped. I, expecting the break, was off before any of them could get to their feet. I got a good distance from them then stopped. I wanted my stuff, but more importantly, I could not leave these people in danger, even Big Nurse. I stood still; Wind found my ear. Yet each time it tried to listen, it also had to ease up on those three and they used each break to advance. Wind hit upon an idea; it would follow and amplify my breath, a great new trick. Of the three only Big Nurse was in a rage. She was the first one I tried it on. A couple of times she strode towards me but I puffed toward her and Wind pushed her back. On her third try, I blew extra hard. Wind swept her off her feet to send her rolling before she crashed into the building so hard I winced. Jess and the other man rushed to her, spoke as they checked her and glanced back at me. I was trying to get wind to understand about the fire when Jess and the other man, both tried flanking runs. I blew out the other much faster man first so Jess got all the closer before I could I face him. He zigged and zagged, took dives, tucked and rolled which is why I missed him twice. He got very close before I blew toward the ground in front of him giving him a blast of dust and gravel right in his face for all his trouble. While he staggered, half blind, coughing and gasping for air, I let him have it again. I stood my ground while the two injured men helped each other walk over to the nurse as she was struggling to stand up. They looked back at me only once with looks of disbelief, anger, and fear all in the mix.

I cared not a wit if they understood what was going on or not; I mean who'd believe them anyway? A couple of persons came out to help them with the nurse but she waved them all off and continued to walk on her own. I looked around; everyone was busy. I finally had a chance to tell Wind what I wanted done about the fire. I hoped it would help. I must have looked like a nut basket to anyone seeing me as I gesticulated and spoke as if to myself.

"Without doubt I can put it out, fun it will be for a friend like me. You will see, as will they, what a friend Wind can be. Yet, do you not want to be free? Do you want to have these men know you have something to do with me?"

"Please Wind, please, help them, they helped me."

"For you alone, I am gone to atone. I will conspire to finish this fire." The air about the whole place grew suddenly still – everyone in the area paused to look up or about in puzzlement. I looked over at the building. The three had come back out and stood near the door to watch me. I wanted to tell them Wind would soon put out the fire yet Wind was right, I had already shown far too much. I was not happy with my talent being exposed so.

I walked back toward the building. They stood aside as I went through the doors. I got all my stuff together. Even as I did so, most of the phone work and radio messaging began to drop off. Without missing a beat, everyone switched gears to all sorts of other work in or around the place. It seemed best to wait, Joey said. I opened a window. I stood by waiting for Wind. I guess I had showed them. I was happy. Now they would see what I could do; they would thank me. I'd go on my way to freedom.

In a few minutes, I heard a helicopter land outside. The way some of the folks acted after a few "suits" stepped out raised my suspicions and my gut turned in fear. However, these suits came in no farther than the foyer, remaining outside the inner set of glass doors. They were not firemen or like anyone else, yet they wore their suits as if they were a uniform. While everyone else inside continued working they called people over, first the head ranger and then El and Jesse. They spoke with each of them in a terse quick way. During those conversations, one or the other of them looked my way; as if I could not see them or understand what was going on. They took Jess, El with a few others outside and then out of sight. They were all probably saying I was one messed up kid, insane or I had delusions or whatever. I did not care what they said. I was scared of this one guy though, the biggest one. He never talked, moved or took off his sunglasses. He stood still the whole time in a set stance as he stared at me.

My time came when the field units began reporting not only was the fire dying down, there was much talk of freak weather conditions. Some reported heavy fog, mists, rain or changes in the wind's direction, which had forced the fire back onto ground already burnt out.

I was daydreaming at a window when Jess suddenly came back inside. I saw his reflection in the glass. I turned to see him striding toward me as El caught up with him, grabbed a hold of his shoulder and forcefully turned him toward her. She gesticulated referencing me, and despite his temper got him to listen to her as she spoke intently, even if in a harsh whisper. He stood stock still for a while as she implored or argued about something. For a moment, they stopped and just stared at each other before he shot an angry glance my way and walked back out with her at his side.

Vehicles began steaming into the area around the building. Lots of people came inside where food was being set out – most all were talking about the weather they'd seen or heard tell of as they checked or signed papers as the emergency forces disbanded. I heard some say a blast of cold wind had broken the main line of the fire with a flurry of snow and hail. The most bizarre was the matter of fact report of a couple of minor tornadoes. They had run up along the main roadways to pretty much clear them of fallen logs, debris and some of the persons making those reports could not shut up about it. Many doubted those reports until more and more eyewitnesses came in to verify those tall tales – and others. Discussion soon switched to attempts at explanation which no one could agree upon and soon everyone expressed relief from the backbreaking work and there were exuberant smiles all around. In a quiet moment, I sidled up beside Jess and, with a bit of pride in my voice, said, "See, I told you the fire would be put out."

He was about to say something, when another urgent call came in over the radio. He took down information and rushed to hand it off before someone told him to go help the ambulances arriving and to remove the severely injured. I did not want to tell him anyway. I decided to get something to eat. Certainly, the fire was dead.

I was eating when Jess walked toward me with another man. Jess introduced me to Mr. Jane. Jess told me I could talk to him about getting free of my parents. I stopped eating and stared up at the well dressed, overweight, squinty eyed, puffy-faced, old white man. He sat down across from me with his own tray of food, which he certainly did not need and certainly did not relish though picked at it nonetheless. He had a nice smell about him. His hands were soft and his nails manicured. He had a gold watch. He said he was a doctor and could see to it I did not have to go home; I could stay at a camp his research and charity organization maintained for children wanting legal separation from their parents. I've to say, he seemed sincere; he even sounded good however I did not need him, really. From the get-go, I only considered him, first and foremost, as a meal ticket and, secondarily, as an easy escape platform. I didn't fully listen any more than I needed save to keep up my lies as he asked questions; it was quite the game, as the man was of inconsiderable intelligence having neither eye to see nor wit to make use of his sight. As we talked, the place began to clear out. "So when can I sign up for this camp of yours." I said, cutting him off and to the chase.

Caught off guard he leaned back seeming to be happy. "Well, as soon as you want. I think we'll need a social worker to let your parent's know then a judge to grant permission.

"How long though?"

"Well, let me make a couple of calls, ok?"

"Ok," I said. I smirked as he lumbered, in his waddling way, to use one of the phones. I noticed he left his tray for someone else to take care of. I stayed by myself, keeping near to an open window.

After a while Jess came back in with a few other rangers. They began to collect and organize a massive pile of paperwork detailing the action taken during the fire. They also had to account for the fact the two fire trucks, weighing 8 tons each, had been carried off by those twisters only to be found set down, fully intact, nearly two miles from any fire road, on a rocky outcrop famed as an overlook not far off one of the more difficult trails.

I was staring off out the window when wind told me it was a funny thing to do. I do not get Wind's sense of humor.

Soon another wave of personnel began arriving and the place was crowded again. These workers had come in from the farther reaches of the park. They had been cut off at one point and nearly lost several of their number. I was surprised they knew about me, how I had worked at the center, was a runaway with some bad luck. To them I was a bit of a celebrity. I had, in the rush of the emergency, made a few good calls, and word about that had gotten around. They gave me a small ranger's hat to wear then proudly dished out some ice cream for me. We mugged it up for some pictures too. It was great. I told them about where I hiked. They laughed about the spring, saying freshets, downhill from a pasture are often contaminated with cow dung, or worse, weed killers and pesticides. Jess showed me a book about camping called: "Months Alone, Easy Survival in the American West." I began to flip through it while Joey, of course, did all the memorizing he wanted. He loves doing that. I told him it looked like a real handy book. One of the men promised to get me a spare copy that he had.

  I will have to leave soon. Mr. Jane worked the radio. He gave me thumbs up. Wind knocked down the telephone lines but cannot stop radio. Mr. Jane says he will have results by tomorrow. He optimistically smiled; he believed I could have my majority. I felt safe. I do not have to worry. I will sleep here tonight then rethink it all in the morning.

5/30/83, Midnight

Dear Joey,

  I read the book most of yesterday as well as pretty much all of today. I feel fine. Big Nurse says I am pretentious. They have not gotten hold of mom or Vince. I've to admit it was strange to hear of my parents camping as the reason they were not reached. I know how Vince likes camping; it could be his one virtue – still it struck me as very odd because the new version of mom hated it.

  I've to get away. I heard three of the friendly rangers talking about going out to check facilities. One of them gave me his copy of that book; I was grateful. I talked to them about taking me on their rounds. Mr. Jane was still working on getting me free of my folks. He said it would be good for me to get some fresh air. I had him believing I'd do anything to keep his trust. He thinks I am dependent on him. That is why he let me go. One of the things the rangers were going to check was a watchtower, a new one, which had not been in the fire's zone; they said it was the tallest in the state.

Still, they had me sleep in that same small room while someone kept an eye on me. The window now had bars on it. Mr. Jane says he wants to be sure I am safe; he says he does not want me to get sick again. The camp doctor says I am not quite well. Even though the fire is out, there are plenty of people around. There are some National Guard troops here too. I overheard one of them say they are going to rebuild some trails or do emergency training.

Late at night, they caught me putting antibiotics with some other medial supplies into my kit when they came to check me. They crazily said I was trying to kill myself. They would not listen when I told them I had read the books on the shelves. I knew I'd need of those things. I didn't say it was because of my escape plans. I told them I'd have left money – this only made them suspicious. They searched my stuff for money they but only Wind knows where it is. However, handy old Mr. Jane, who had listened patiently, defended me. He calmed the situation down. When we were alone, he told me I could, in the presence of a judge or a military officer in charge of an emergency scene, sign my own papers. I could be granted a self-directed guardianship as soon as tomorrow when the commander of the National Guard unit arrived. I was wary but pretended excitement. I got Mr. Jane to tell me wonderful things about his camp – Joey and I dreamt to it, it was a prison camp, no one was happy there, not even the guards or Mr. Jane.

5-30-83

Dear Joey,

The next day two rangers came by with a man from the energy department. They took me out. We rode through camping areas then ate pancakes with some lumberjacks harvesting fallen trees. We looked over water systems, a road clearing operation before hiking off to measure the pond behind a beaver dam. I had a truly odd feeling, off and on, all the while. I felt watched. The sense was odd maybe not a person or not wholly a person, very odd.

The last thing was to check in at a watchtower. As we drove toward its location, I felt it might be a perfect launch point for a getaway – there would only be the three of them plus whoever was in the tower. I was going to be about as far away as I could get from anything. The fire road was long, bumpy, and dusty thus I could not talk to the Wind. My regret would be the loss of my stuff. Without saying as much, I had left it there as a demonstration of trust to a proudly smiling Mr. Jane. All the while Joey was quiet. I had no way of knowing if Mr. Jane planned to return me to my parents or what. I knew he was lying, one way or another. Joey had said they could be flown here, which meant I could be back with them as soon as tomorrow. Further, on the bad side, none of the men were ever very far away from me. Even when I took a pee, someone stayed right nearby, on the other side of the tree.

The tower was impressive; it was over 300 feet tall and perched on a rocky outcrop of a ridge near the south end of the park. It had a field of vision covering many thousands of square miles and a very unusual array of antennas.

There were several men inside which was disappointing, in terms of my intent to escape. They let me use a telescope. They let me look over a few of their special maps. Joey took due notes. As they got down to business, I had a chance to be still enough to talk with Wind.

They had their backs to me as they gathered around a table and a bunch of electronic gear along the wall. I positioned myself for a break. I was all set when a car's horn sounded below. Someone they knew was coming up. I heard it was an Indian, a real one. I put off my plans for a moment. I wanted to see what he was like.

He was a big man, barrel-chested, with thick long black hair tied tightly at the back of his head, a broad face with deep set features, and bright, quick, assertive eyes. He looked very much like someone I had seen in books though even Joey couldn't recall details, the name nor tribe for that matter, that was way odd. He talked to the others about work on the ridge road where heavy equipment was moving in.

When we ate lunch, he talked with me, briefly. He was Ohlone, a tribe still living in the Bay Area, although most of his known relatives lived in the southwest. That's when Joey made things difficult. He began to speak in the man's native language as I was talking. I had learned my lesson on that score; I didn't want trouble. Joey kept on though, which made it hard to listen to him while he babbled. When the man asked a question, I blurted something out, just a few words, lies of course, but it wasn't English, and I never saw a such a look as the one he gave me, not only did he look as if he could listen, I mean as Joey or the Wind could – but I surely felt the stare of his eyes! Joey got scared. So, when he asked if I knew what I had said, I looked away. I lied about hearing tape somewhere and deciding to ask him if he knew what it meant. He only looked down before asking about me. I told him I was the Long Runaway and that I had helped out at the center during the fire. He looked me again – this time he put impressive power into it. Boy oh boy, what a set of eyes! I had to look away – or tell the truth – just, as it seemed, he did. We finished eating in silence. He got up without looking back, said his farewells to the others and left.

When they settled down to work, I got ready and, to myself, I mumbled, "Well, here goes nothing." I ran for it. I had not noticed one of the men had gone outside. He caught me easily and set me back down – inside.

I turned to them saying what Joey had me say, except loud. "I am going to go away, I don't want to go home; you can't make me." I still was not sure I could get away without hurting them. They looked at me from the table because I had spoken loud enough that they couldn't ignore it.

"Look, kid, you have to stay with us for now, maybe your parents will come for you or maybe you'll go with that guy, what's his name, Jane. All we want is for you to be happy, kid. Just cool off, huh"

"I'm not going to go back to them ever." I had to say what Joey would not. He believed it would be easier to go back to them and start all over by escaping from them but I didn't want to go through that mess again.

"Look, kid." One of the rangers got up then started to move toward me, while the other man remained blocking the doorway. "We only want to help you, you see..."

"You can help me by letting me go with all my stuff."

"Well, that's interesting, where does a what, nine year old, come up with enough money to stay out, as you have, and keep supplied, and get some nice gear – that's what I'd like to know. I mean to say, less than a hundred dollars were taken from your home when you left, you've been on your own for a while, and you don't look like you can do any real work. So why don't you tell me about that?" Another ranger had moved forward from my left while the man at the door was hunkering down, I could feel it. No slipping out; I was surrounded. The man behind me said, "How can you get away, you gonna fly out of here?"

"The same way I stopped the fire."

The man in front of me became incredulous, mocking. Standing above me making gestures to mimic mine as he said, in sotto voice, "The same way I stopped the fire." They all laughed. I felt a pit of weirdness in my stomach. I was solid, cold frightened – and looked it.

Another ranger asked, "What did you have that a few thousand men did not have?"

I raised my arm dramatically, "The same thing I will use right now if you don't let me out of here, pronto." They looked at me as if I was some little nut as the mocker mocked me, imitating my feeble gestures and phrases in a falsetto voice.

"Ah the kid is nuts," said another. He was tired and said, "Look, Mark, talk some sense into him. I'm not getting readings right now, so I don't know what to tell you anyway." One of the others said, "Why not take him outside, see what happens if he cools his jets a bit."

"Sure, will do,"

"You want to sit outside for a while?"

In silence, we went out. We sat near the doorway on a built in bench and it wasn't long before he started in, "Listen, we don't have anything against you, ok? We want to help. If you can't get along with your parents, the law looks into the mess. Besides, you got sick. It's not good you should go around like that. What if you had broken a leg? Why not wait a few years; you'll be able to go wherever you want with no one to tell you different." Mark was earnest. He seemed, at that moment, to care. He talked in a hushed tone so only he and I could hear even though the others were still inside at the table continuing to talk about instrument readings as they adjusted settings on instruments. Mark made sense except everything he said led to me going with some adult. He told me he'd run away when he was kid, staying out for three weeks. First, I knew he was lying; second, even if he was not, just because he got in trouble did not mean I would. After all, I had Joey and Wind. It certainly did not help his argument when he talked about getting back to my school and friends.

"Ok, let's just pretend that it was really nice, quite nice." I interrupted. "What does that matter if I don't want to go back?"

He looked at me, tipped back his hat and spoke slowly, "Look, one way or another the authorities are going to take care of you. Now, it may be Mr. Jane, or someone like him, a Youth Guidance center, a half way house. I only want you to be happy, that's all." He looked me in straight in eyes. He blinked first.

"I still won't go."

"I'm afraid the law says different. Kid you're too young to be out on your own. Besides, you're famous; someone will always spot you. Do you want to live a hard life on the road, on the run always looking out or in hiding? Like I say, go to high school then take off. You do have a lot of time, I wish that I had your chances, boy I'd do things different, why you know…" Annoyingly he went on about how he would have done this, certainly not that, and ended by saying hindsight is golden. I listened for a minute or two. When he paused – that was my chance.

"I know you want to help me. It is no use. You do not understand."

He opened his mouth to object. I cut him short. "You listen to me I am going to show you now." I sat still and whispered for Wind; it was there in an instant; it had never left. I looked at unsuspecting man and smiled broadly.

"Tell them to stop what they are doing. I am going to show you all what I can do."

"Come on kid, they are doing work, leave them alone – show me, ok?" I've to say he certainly looked like he cared. I agreed; I had him stand up and take a few long steps away.

"Watch," I said.

He stood there, hands on the railing, looking out as if he expected nothing. A sudden forceful blast of air completely knocked him off his feet; he landed flat on his back with a resounding thud. In the quiet, the others inside noticed. I heard them exclaim. One of them stuck his head out to check. He walked out as Mark tried to tell him a microburst had caught him off guard. Just as the other man began to laugh and chide him, a powerful blast slammed him up against the wall pressing him onto it. I signed and the wind cut out off. The man slumped onto the deck and then both of them got up but they were dazed. Amazingly, they talked about freak winds.

"I did that that, me. Hey, listen to me."

Mark was impatient. "Listen kid, maybe you need some kind of help. You know someone to talk to, someone who will listen…"

As the others came out excitedly, Wind forced them all back inside. It carried off all their papers far, far away only to let them sprinkle into the trees. It set up a powerful current of air that whined as it closely circled the tower without so much as touching it or moving the nearby trees. None of them said a word as they marveled at a filmy, glistening wall of air.

I went up to each of them, looked them in the eye as I spoke to Mark about how, at a signal, Wind would let up and that would be that. I gave that signal; the Wind let off. I did not know what to say, except the obvious. They looked at me with stony faces, I had their attention, I said, "I want to go my own way."

"I can't let that happen, you know that," said John, a big man. Without him saying so, I knew he was the boss by the way they deferred to him; the only thing they didn't do was salute.

"Well, I think you are wrong. What about it, huh, big boss man?"

"Why you little bastard! I'm gonna … " John snarled as he started after me. The phrase was never finished. The wind broke in, seized him up and pressed him against the ceiling until the place began to shake as if it would break apart. He was suffocating. I signed before I could speak, Wind cut off. He fell like a rock, out cold before hitting the floor. The others did CPR; it was touch and go. I was scared more than ever. Thankfully, he came to and seemed all right. The others, Mark included, busied themselves with taking care of John even as they stayed clear of me. I walked toward the doorway.

"You will let me go. You should see that by now."

They all looked at me though, as if planning something. I signaled, as the howling began they cringed as they cast glances about until, at a gesture, the howling stopped. Mark advanced with one of the others until a pronounced gust pushed them both back. As soon as they stopped trying to advance, Wind ceased.

"What in God's name are you?" Mark trembled, hardly able to speak clearly yet unable to contain the question; they all started shouting not questioning so much as venting anger in a mad demanding sort of babble. I did not have to call on the Wind. When I raised my hand, they shut their gobs but quick.

"It does not matter. I do not have to say a thing. I want to go and you," I pointed to John, "You will take me back to the camp. I want to get my stuff then get out of here." He looked around; no one volunteered to take his place.

"Ok, ok, I'll do it. I don't see as there is much else to do. You guys try to get the equipment recalibrated. That'll do for now." He looked at me. "That's ok isn't it?"

"Sure, that's ok. I do not want to mess with anyone's work, sorry about the papers. You go down first."

"Ok?"

Neither of us said a word. My main concern was I had used Wind right in front of them in ways they could not deny. There was little profit in arguing with them or waiting for another time. As my mom would say, "What's done is done."

We got into the camp. He, he hopped out but Wind slowed him right down. I told him to stay where he was and that "the wind is watching. If you so much as move, that will be it." I drew my index finger across my throat. He stopped and looked all about at the clear air then up into the clouds.

As I entered, everyone stopped and stared. I strolled calmly to where I had left my stuff, gathered it all up and went right back out without so much as a how do you do. I keep forgetting about radio. The guys at the tower must have told them to expect me and to let me do as I wanted. I didn't see Mr. Jane, but that was fine. John drove me out to the border of the park, uneventfully. I told him to drive to San Jose, not to turn back or stop anywhere along the way. I told him Wind would get him if he did not do as I said. To make my point, a breeze came up to rock his vehicle. John simply drove off.

Later I found out my parents were notified and had been on their way even as I escaped according to the papers anyway.

I walked the rest of the day staying well off any road. I found a campsite. I worked on writing this account. Sleep was never so inviting, God Bless those less fortunate.

I know that I am alone. I will keep it that way. No one can get near me now. All I have to do is keep Wind with me. As for Mr. Jane's camp, Wind went there and broke down the fencing but only a few escaped, most were totally brainwashed, amazing.

5/31/83

Dear Joey,

I walked all day. I eked my way along. It was great getting to the ocean. I found a place on a beach where I set stuff out like a picnic. I swam a good deal before drying off. I took time searching for a place to camp.

I plan to go south. I still have a lot of money. I keep reading the ranger's book. There are ways to keep safe. I know many of the medical plants now. I know I've been lucky too. The good thing is that there is food all around as I go.

6/1/83

Dear Joey,

It is June first as I move south. This is the greatest. I am free to go anywhere I want. Last night, for the first time, Joey and Wind were in my dream. We went out over the Pacific Ocean as if we were invisible gliders. We saw islands and went lower to watch fishermen in hand made boats. We flew around them as if we were birds and, for a minute, stood upon the roughly hewn wooden deck of one of their catamarans. They began to play music and sing. We liked these guys! I got inside one. He was a good drummer, a little drunk but very happy. They had circular nets, which they flung out over the water in order to catch fish. Well, Wind and I went into the water and herded the fish, all that we could instigate, into their nets. You should have seen it. They never had so many fishes at one time. They were laughing so hard they lost almost half of them.

Tahiti is beautiful. I may go there someday. We stayed at the top of one of the big mountains to watch the sunset in the Pacific. Joey told me stories about the place. Starting with the way people used to live there. It is different now. They have cars, busses, an army, policemen, hotels, and garbage. The ocean is nice though as are the beaches.

Just as Joey can read well and remember after just glimpsing a page, I can draw pictures of the places I see. All I've to do is close my eyes and trace from the memory. Well, I've to open my eyes in order to see the page every once in a while before closing my eyes to see the image, so it is almost like tracing. Santa Cruz is the next big town. I want to buy some paper, coloring pencils. I'd like to send a post card home, maybe.

Like always, I keep off highways, walk through fields, and edge around farms. I found a good watch. Now I will know what time it is.

If I do not get to Santa Cruz tonight, I will have to camp without a fire, unless I can get real far from people.

Wind brought papers. There is a big reward from my parents for anyone who finds me. I do not see how Vince or mom could get that kind of dough, unless they had help. I do not care. I am going on.

I asked Wind if there was anyone else it talks to.

"No one, child. You are all for me, my friend along with the earth and the sea."

Wind said our friendship had ameliorated the various impossibilities inherent in our relationship, using even more big words I had to learn from Joey. I pretended to understand. I nodded and forgot about it.

Wind said I taught it a lot. It had wondered about cigarettes, for example. I explained how although people seemed to like them even thought they were bad for health and that people had a hard time quitting. Wind learned why cars smell so awful bad, what airplanes and windows were and came to understand factories. It described what could only be war and when I tried to explain that, I did not do very well at all.

I camped out. I wrote by flashlight. I took out my ring and looked at it. The stone was dark as always although, earlier in the day, I had felt it at my heart as a tingling, or an ache or longing, even an itch but inside it was something like all of those or none; you know? Anyway, Joey said if I waited until dark to look at a candle through its gemstone, I'd learn something. Joey was being dumb again. When I told him he got mad and went away. Even in the daylight, the thing is nearly opaque. I mean when I looked straight through it at the sun all I saw it was a mix of dark green colors, a glint of deep blue, a red or red-brown along with a few slashes of yellow-gold; you could hardly see the sun's light. I had to apologize to Joey though. A few minutes ago, when I tried it, he was right. For a blink or two, I saw an Indian walking along a path. That was it. It was as if I had deeply dreamt by looking through the stone. I asked Wind. It only said the ring was old. That I should scrub it clean tomorrow in stream water to see it for what it was. Well no more for tonight, I am overtired and going to sleep.

6/3/83

Dear Joey,

I am staying in the hills for now. Yesterday I decided to risk crossing a freeway otherwise I'd have to go maybe a couple of miles to get to an irrigation ditch, which went under it. What do you know but a CHP car was within shouting distance. As it slowed down, I ran off.

I hopped a fence and ran through a field of cherry tomatoes before heading toward some trees. I looked back. The officer had not moved. He was speaking into his radio's microphone. Of course, when I got near enough to the other side of the trees, I snuck along while peeking through the roadside underbrush. Sure enough, a police car was idling along less than a hundred yards from where I stood. I had to dash across the road. If I stayed put, they would have known exactly where I was, even if they did not know I was the runaway.

This second officer got out and gave chase. I had to run like heck through a field of strawberries barely keeping ahead of him. I could not raise the wind so I was panicking. After I made it out of the field and into the countryside, I was able to get some cover behind bushes or circle around behind rocky outcrops. For a while, it was hide and seek. Although he got close a few times, he was never close enough. I could not raise Wind; I did not dare whistle it up either – our newest emergency signal. We would have to make another.

I heard him hollering over to some one. I knew he was not alone and that I was less safe. I scrambled to top a high hill's ridge. There was another roadway on the other side. Waiting there was police vehicle with a couple of officers on dirt bikes beside it. Beyond them was an expanse of row crops. This was all great – to top it off I could not raise Wind. It had been silent and I did not know where my enemy was.

I wondered how they knew where I was so quickly. It sure looked like a set up. However, for the life of me, I could not figure how they set it up.

Then "Mr. Legs," as I had come to call him, began calling me by name, so they had me figured and trapped. Why else would he give away his position by calling out so? I moved down the ridge keeping hidden from those on the road below while using Mr. Leg's voice to keep tabs on him. As long as they did not see me, I had a still had chance to sidle out of this mess and slide on down the road, or trail.

I crawled carefully gaining distance from the officers on the road. I was getting to think I had shaken Mr. Legs when I heard his voice from somewhere out in front of me. He was directing the others. The dirt bikes started up. They would be up here in no time. I took a big risk then and peeked over a rock. I saw "Legs" had his back to me. I could hear the motorbikes closing so I took a big fat risk and scuttled up over a large boulder, in plain sight, before easing myself down its far side, onto another's curved surface, and then hunkered down in a shadowy crevice between a couple of others. I heard Legs call but it seemed as though he was farther off. I carefully reached out to pull in some dry brush to set it up in front of me. Those, plus the tall grasses, and shrubs made a great blind. Ironically, from my position, atop a small group of hills rising out of the valley floor, although I could readily see the display of ranches and distant traffic on the two lane roads crisscrossing the valley, I was blind to my immediate surroundings. To the east, there was a line of trees which wandered in slow curves along it length. It must be a creek, maybe something bigger though it offered no hope of escape; it was too far away. I carefully called Wind.

"Oh, you are under stress, I guess, yes?"

"Oh thank you, thank you. I need help, I want to be alone, can you see a way out or which way to go?"

"No, No you cannot go. More than one is in your way, others are coming closer to where you stay, and you're their prey."

This struck me down; what could I do? Legs had to be closing. I still had to rest before darting out yet I had no idea as to which way or to where. The farms around here all grew short row crops; there was nothing like corn wherein I could hide. From where I sat, behind my blind of shrubs and grasses, Legs was using tracking strategies I'd seen in the ranger's book. He was circling back and not far away. Down below on the road a semi trailer approached the police position. As it passed along side, the police car flipped over and rolled down the sloping shoulder. The sound of its explosion distracted Mr. Legs. He ran off to look. The truck was weaving away erratically; the police car was in flames while its two officers lay flat on the asphalt. Legs rushed off, no longer concerned with me. I knew what had happened. Wind had used the big truck as a disguise and it hadn't hit the car. I could see the officers were moving but struggling to get up. I couldn't hear the dirt bikes so maybe wind did something to them too. I just hoped it wasn't obvious; I didn't want to leave any more evidence.

I did not like hurting anyone nor did wind so I was sure no one was. I guess Wind knew best. I told it to put the car's fire out so it would not start any others. I left on the quick. If I go into town, I will have to be careful.

Later, the newspapers Wind brought did not have any information about my parents. I ate and slept very well. I looked into my ring again seeing the Indian before I saw a group of men looking over papers. I did not know them. I sensed they were very far away and talking about me even though I could not hear them, which was odd. They each spoke different languages but understood each other well enough. There were other quick images too, a snowy blizzard, a machine, a large array of towers with lights, then more men talking, some in uniforms. I could not understand what they were saying, even though I believed it was my own language. The Indian came back into focus. He was slowly walking along a highway but when I saw a billboard I remembered laughing at, I knew he was about two days behind me. He seemed to look right up at me; I mean, right at me through the ring, and nod. I saw him leave the road right away. He was changing direction. I was convinced I had given him a clue, Joey argued with me saying it was impossible. I got madder than I've ever been at him when he would not shut up about it. I decided to keep moving after dinner. When I stopped, I did not make a real camp.

After some hours, Joey finally admitted the Indian was following. I do not want to listen to him. I do not have to since Wind is with me. Also, I do not understand him sometimes – he jokes around a lot or argues just to argue. Ever since I did not go home when I was sick he started to be troublesome. He was never like this before. I do not let him read my diary anymore. I think he is mad since Wind showed him he was wrong about the Indian getting a clue about our location after we used the ring. It is annoying to have this problem along with the others. I can avoid people though it is sometimes hard but as to this here Indian, who is he and how is he following me, even along streets and why do I keep getting him on my ring?

Every time I peek at him, he is watching the ground as he walks or standing still looking skyward.

The ring is fascinating, it can be a kind of telephone or camera and, using the ring, I can sense persons I know or those that know of me. I was holding the ring up to my eye looking through the loop, as I thought of a long lost friend. Then, poof, I saw him, well sort of. First, it looked as if I was shining a light around in a very dark room. Then my beam was on him; he was naked, hunkered down, and facing away from me. He jumped up when the light touched on him as if shocked. I had a sense the kid was up inside his own head right behind his own eyes and had been looking out of them. I took his place and lived his life for a few minutes. I was he. It was weird.

I am better at it now. I enter a mind quietly, sense how they are feeling, get an impression of what they are doing and slowly, as if in a dream, see what they do and hear what they hear. Now, I do not need papers to learn about mom. She is ok. It is very tiring to look through the ring; I've a hard hunch it can be dangerous too.

6/5/83, The Indian

Dear Joey,

Wind cannot tell where the Indian is or how far away; it says it seems as if he cannot be seen, which had Joey and Wind agree, for once, on just one thing – he sure was strange.

I feel he is close which is enough to keep me going hard. I am not at all afraid. I do not want to hurt anyone or bother anyone. When will everyone leave me alone? What am I doing anyway? All I want to do is walk around and take care of myself, is that a crime? I mean why, why, why, why, why, why why, why, why and dagnabit, dingblast – why? Darn it!

Wind believes the Indian is not close enough to find me though it is surprised to see how he keeps coming along. Since he seems old, he must have some inner strength or tremendous motivation. I can't figure how he can track me when Wind takes care of any trace of my passing or when I walk along on pavement or along in a stream. I'd certainly like to learn what he knows – boy, now that would be great!

I'd also like to know how he travels with just about nothing on him except his clothes. He does not have a pack or keep food on him. I figure he must be going on what he finds. He never builds a fire.

Last night I had Wind help me as I dreamt. We went looking for him for what seemed like hours. We could not find him so I used the ring in the dream and we found him or rather where we knew him to be but his location was hidden. In the dream state all I cold see was a bubble of thick fog over a wide area that encompassed where we knew him to be. It was blurry and wiggly at the same time. We left off the search and puzzled over this new phenomenon.

Then, as I looked back to the area where he was, I had Wind blow, not enough to carry off a man, but surely enough to move things around. In a moment, the mystery area cleared and we went back to see him chasing around gathering up some little stones, incense sticks, and a few articles of clothing. I was giggling, when he stopped, turned to look up as if he could see through the ring's view and then I seemed to be pulled into his glaring right eye. I dropped the ring I was so scared. I didn't want to believe I had seen him before but Joey, "the disagreeable one" insisted I'd met him at the tower. I knew he was right but I wouldn't admit it. I did not want to hurt him. I was glad he seemed ok and that I could slow him down. I was not sure what else I should do even but I figured he was no more than 40 miles away.

This morning I took the time to write down the last few days. Sorry if they appear scattered. I do not want anyone following – that's that. I do not know if he is a danger, an annoyance, or what. I cannot figure him out. He certainly knows how to hide and can track a fish upstream or down as they say.

6/10/83

Dear Joey,

I got close to town. I wanted to go take care of my clothes, buy a note pad, some pencils, and maybe have a hot meal, steak with home fried potatoes.

I was well into the outskirts of a suburb, when I chanced upon a bus stop and decided to ride into town both to save time and lessen the chance of being seen. However, this suburb was a real fancy. I felt I stood out like a sore thumb. I joined the people waiting at a stop. Cautiously, as ever, I turned away to draw out some money. I did not want anyone to see what I had on me. When the bus came, I let all the older people on first then paid as the bus started moving.

When I turned to go down the aisle however, I saw the Indian. I nearly jumped out of my skin and lost my footing but he was fast asleep thank god. The people looked askance at me as I hurried past them to sit as far back as I possibly could. I feared my commotion would wake him though after I was safely sitting, I saw he had not stirred. I pretended to nap as I watched him from my dreams. I even used the ring but I did not go inside his head.

He was definitely sleeping, his head leaned against the window – even the occasional jolt did not rouse him. He slept the whole time. I began to worry about the best place to get off. I did not want to wait until he got off; he might look around and see me. On the other hand, if I waited too long, he might see me as I got off. When the bus got to an area of older warehouse businesses, railroad tracks, in a worn out industrial area, I got off because it was the kind of area I could move around in without looking suspect. I got off by the back doors. I kept thinking I could not wait to grow up; if I were 10 years older even five, I'd have no problems. I could go anywhere or do anything, really.

At the first gas station I came across, I used the men's room. In a flat 10 minutes I had washed up, changed into my remaining clean clothes, and repacked my gear. I weighed buying new duds but food was the first thing on my mind. I went to a café to have a righteous meal. I bought a pencil with a good pad of paper. Soon after, I got into a motel much the same way as I'd gotten in to other places. This time I arrived in a taxi wearing a nametag while acting very innocent. I got in with no trouble. The credit card I got from Wind worked as Joey said it would and would be good for a few days.

I settled into my room. TV sure is stupid, especially the game shows, oh my God! I fell asleep only to wake a few hours later. I decided to go to the little restaurant on the ground floor of the place for some ice cream. When I felt how nice the air was, I decided to go for a walk. I felt I could enjoy some peace and quiet. I went a few blocks. It sure was nice enough however I started to get hungry.

As I approached the restaurant, I saw a man exit a phone booth a half a block ahead. No matter that his back was to me, the light poor, or that he headed off in a hurry – I knew it was the Indian and he was so close that if he had turned around I'd have had to hide behind a car or something. I turned and walked quickly from the scene. I turned a corner then began jogging toward a residential area. I went a few dozen blocks before heading back toward the restaurant and from another direction. I looked before I went around every corner, kept to whatever shadows or cover I could as I meandered to some extent. It was a couple hours before I saw my lodgings again. I worked my way into a shadowy area across the street to wait. It was a sweet spot. I could still see my door and the street in front. I wanted to get inside without any company.

I saw him stroll along in front of the place. He did not look up or around either. I had the advantage. I knew what he looked like and could bet he would not know me from Adam. Well, I mean he might remember me from the tower but I don't think he would know I was the one he was tracking – how could he? Then again, this guy was good. Something had to be done. I wanted to be alone. I had hoped to have a rest without worrying for a few days. Oh well.

I waited; the air got colder. I was feeling safe so I stepped out, cautiously looking around. He was nowhere in sight. I stared across the street. Darn it, if I was not dead sure I was watched even if from far away, very far. I kept my cool though. I strolled into the hotel's restaurant to have an ice cream. When I went back outside, I felt safe. I went for a ways, stopped, whispering to let Wind know I might need it soon.

"Please be free, I will see, you can go here and there for I am aware, I am aware."

I walked around window-shopping. I bought a big chocolate chip cookie acting as I thought a runaway might. I felt I was drawing him on.

It got very late. I kept walking. I knew he was following. The only worrying aspect was, from what I could sense, he had not been the one who'd watched me cross the street earlier. I sensed an astringent quality, a sterile chill about whoever, or whatever that was but there was no sense of it now.

Still, I was curious about the Indian, as I became the hunter. I began to search for a likely alleyway. When I found one, I passed it by at first only to double back suddenly as to catch sight of him, about half block away. He suddenly turned to his right acting as though he had wanted to cross in the middle of the block. He did not look my way as I stood there, looking around, pretending to be undecided. I waited until he started putting distance between us at which time I began to doubt his intent. Even after he was out of sight, I knew he was never far away, a few blocks, I could feel it. After a time, when I knew he was again closing, I went down another alley. I had him.

I walked more slowly, stopped, and turned shouting, "Why are you following me?" but I took a couple steps back, shocked to see was he was so darned close – not ten feet back!

Bravely, I repeated my emphatic demand as he looked around. First, expectantly back toward the alley's opening as if looking for back up or to see if someone had heard me. I pointed. Wind picked up enough to puff him back a few steps. This was enough to frighten him, sure. He tried to move away. It was my turn now. Wind shoved him hard this way and that until he stopped trying to move. He was mine.

"Why are you following me?" He was scared. I wanted him to feel it for a while. I demanded he tell me what was going on, was he part of a group, did someone send him and, if so, who? I told him I wanted a simple way of living. I did not want his problems along with mine. Inside I was scared. I kept thinking I might have to kill him if he was dangerous. I worried about what kind of life such an act would make for me. I know you are not supposed to kill; it is wrong, always. No one should kill anyone no matter what, everyone has a right to life – though, I guess, some do have to be forced to stop doing bad things and then into being helped. I stared at him. Wind hummed around him a shiny, whirling yet silent wall.

Finally, in stuttered language, he began to talk even as he looked around marveling at what he saw.

"I wander around, take odd jobs, ranch hand, harvest vegetables, and some times work fairs, or at amusement parks. You go to amusement parks; I know I saw you do some tricks at Great America ..." I said nothing to him, using my best poker stare. "... and at revivals. I know that you find things in the wind. Then, I had a calling to wander and then to follow something and it turned out that it was you. That's how I came to be at the park and get hired on temporary. When fire broke out, they took me on full time. At that time I didn't know it was you I was tracking. Look, you and I got no one. I know how the world is, my father told me stories. He told stories about the wind but nothing he said prepared me to see what I saw it do. The wind put out that fire; I swore it. No one believed me; they called me crazy as well as other things. Since I am native, I am used to the insults, depreciation or the outright disdain of the invaders. Soon, everyone thought everyone else was crazy for what they said they saw. I wondered about you at the tower with the rangers, I knew there was something up because there was a certain government man there. Just as I knew he would not remember me, I was a boy when I last saw him, so I knew some kind of big-time lie was going on. I did not think it had to do with you, I believed they were doing something with the weather. You see, I know someone who helped construct the watchtower months before and I was there when the tower got a delivery of more electronic gear than I've ever seen. A helicopter, a big military model with government markings, brought it all in, just before the fire. So I just plain worked dumb to plumb it and plumb it I did. What I noticed were the inconsistencies between what they said they were doing and what I knew some of the devices were used for. When I saw you there, I heard something. I did not know what, like a whisper – except big. After I left, a crazy kind of storm caught me."

"When I got back to the command center, I heard the story about the runaway. The nurse, for one, was very clear. I overheard her talking; that's when I knew you had something. Later, when the same guy interviewed everyone who had seen you, even me – well it was odd. I mean they had a team of persons asking questions, not regular questions. For example I understood they had the book on me and no matter what I said someone was going to check everything. A few of the questions were pointedly about you and what I knew about you. My thinking was they'd gotten you to that tower to record what you do or map it somehow so I went back to see what I could do – by that time you were long gone. I knew you were in a kind trouble you didn't know about. I made motions to the four directions, I wafted my prayer incense and followed, not because you need me but because they're after you and you needed to know that at least. You can't live in their world anymore, you need to learn to survive."

I told him I trusted him. I felt good about him in a way that was interesting. I did not tell him about the ring, which was warm to me and so I felt he was telling his truth. I was going to ask him to walk along with me.

"No, wait, let me finish. The most important thing is you. You can learn the way. You have to. You know the Wind. Yes, I know, I know. I needed to believe. Now, I do. That's important. I had to know. My sadness is I cannot sing of this while knowing what it means, perhaps, my time is near. I have to help."

"How do you trail me, so well?"

"I learned pathways from all my family and relations. I can listen to the sun and moon; the earth tells tales of all travelers, birds talk and plants listen."

"I saw you long before you got near me." I was not about to tell him how even though I had decided to trust him.

It was hard for him to talk so I signaled Wind to ease up. This allowed him to relax, although there was still was a force rushing about him, his clothes and hair were in constant yet slight motion while only a few feet away on the ground, papers and trash were motionless.

"What is your name?"

"I am not easy with my name. What's yours?"

"I am not easy with my name either."

We stood there in silence, neither wanting to admit our names to the other. "I do not think you're bad. Maybe you do not belong to any group nor are you an actor. I do not want you to follow me. I do not have to trust anyone, you know that as well as I. I can get along myself, without any aid."

"You got sick."

"Bad water, I know about such things now."

"They want you."

"I can be careful from now on."

"You are too young, you need to grow to an adult. You may never make it. I couldn't stand for that to happen again after waiting so many cent..." He stopped himself from saying something else, apparently worse that what he just said, "I mean to say, not … uh … this time – with one of us, my family I mean, standing nearby. The enemy will always be after you, if you don't give them what they want. I know."

"The President…"

"He does not know everything."

"What do you mean?"

"The enemy is deeply planted, very strong with many hands, eyes, and feet. It is not seen for what it is; it hides in the open. It is heartless, ancient and wants to gain the world for its own. It plays with nations as toys."

"Who are they?"

"I don't know names; as well as I know wars, greed or corruption – all their hallmarks."

He was not pleading for himself; he was still terrified while completely in my control. I could see his well-muscled strength was a result of hard work, though his manner was gentle. He, a stranger, was worried about me. I flexed. Wind pressed on him. He closed his eyes, began praying silently, moving only his lips – helpless. He did not beg or try for time. He accepted.

I eased off. We sat down, right where we were, to talk. I felt sure he would still follow and, despite the wind, succeed. Perhaps the government, if it were interested in me, would in turn follow him – I did not state as much, knowing he'd simply nod

I listened as he talked about how he followed me. I was amazed at how many insects were snacks. No wonder he had no pack. Joey noted everything he said, especially about trails or trailing. Wind learned how to erase tracks even better. Best of all I saw how not to leave so many. I bet he could teach me much more. He said, again, something about how he didn't want me to die out before I was truly born; he couldn't stand to see such a thing again." This time I knew what he meant as soon as he said it. I had never thought of it before – how some things need to carry on. In mid-sentence, Wind whooshed up around him, lifting him slightly up off his feet. I felt Wind's power with a feeling of intense, dizzy happiness. I held him in the air and said:

"I want you to teach me. Wind watches over me all the time. You, knowing this, can be trusted your problem will be trusting me – so we can be partners, yes?"

Unable to speak, he nodded an affirmative. I let him down. Wind left. With the weather calm and the night quiet, he said, "Lets get out of town." Without a further word, or gesture, he walked past without a glance. Before we left town, I sent a letter home telling them I was ok and they did not have to worry. I told them I'd come home when I felt safe. That night he showed me how pack, adjust what I carried; it was great!

6/16/83

Dear Joey,

This is good. We have been walking for three days. He does not let up but laughs, saying, "Fine thing, you can't keep up with an old man, hah!"

I showed him how Wind brings me money with newspapers; he was darned surprised. He did not like the way I made fire or left things around for Wind to take care of. He began to show me how to do such things simply – always aiming to save time or energy. I saw how my little campfires must have given me away. I was so unaware; now I learn all along the day.

He says, with practice we should cover 40 miles a day calling it "slacker easy." Considering all the while I've been out, I've only gone about twice that far, I've my doubts. He says I will like new places. Finally, with an adult, I will be taken for what I appear to be without being hassled for it. I will be able to get along on a lot less money if I learn from him. He says he will teach me to fish, maybe hunt though he prefers foraging for field salads since they can assembled as we go. I am learning about each plant we use such as that one with leaves you use to make a soapy lather.

I do not have time to write much in the diary. I do not care nor does Joey. He says this man is more important.

I began calling him Chief. Although he said nothing about this at first, after while I could sense he was annoyed. We argued for hours. I became stubbornly insistent, as did he. He can argue all he wants. He certainly fits the bill for being MY chief. After all, he was in command, a teacher as well as an elder. He fended off such attempts until I said if he were to take me to his people and I lived among them and "didn't die out" he would certainly be my elder. He said "so."

"So. "I added, "If we moved on, created a new branch, well he would be a chief. " That got him good and quiet for once. I mean to say he mulled for more than an hour.

He fell into telling stories about a kind of tree, rock, or of rivers. Everything has a story. Although I have a sneaking suspicion, now and then, when I think he's making things up, at least in part, but I usually find something to think about or I get curious. Before I know it, I am learning again as we're talking, talking, talking. We never seem to stop. It is as he says, "you'll never loose weight by flapping yer yap flapper".

Still, we are always in a hurry. He wants to go back to see his father and family; says I can learn much more from the others; they will help us keep safe. I agreed that it was worth our while. If they knew my story, they might have second or third thoughts. He insists they will accommodate me on his word alone. It must be good to have a nice, real family.

We are making 25 plus miles a day now. We got pine nuts, some seeds; honey and concocted a kind of savory bullion. He figures, once we hit our stride, we will get there in maybe six or eight weeks at the longest to get there. It is not as far as it sounds. We are going to walk the whole way keeping clear of people along with their troubles. I am eager to learn. Joey helps when he can or wants to. He mostly remembers the stories word for word. He says it is easy, like rereading a book or looking at pictures. Joey always did like stories.

Last night he told us a long, long story about the beaver making all the land there is. The eagle helped, as did the otter, although not very well and mostly by accident, when he played too much causing good luck to spring out of nowhere. All the animals got involved, one way or another. Each showed their respective characteristics as they did so. In the end, they all gave respect to beaver by leaving him alone to do his work – most of the time anyway. My friend can do all the animal's voices; he is good at that. He can do bird whistles too; I am going to learn a few.

I retold one of the first stories he told me. Joey helped me remember. I've not told him about Joey so he thinks I am a fast learner.

Tomorrow we strike out further southeast. This will be the first day we step up to 35 plus miles. A good portion of it is flat though it will be hot which means we'll have to watch water. My hiking shoes are pretty well broken in. We doctored them up, inside and out. Now, I packed light with a tight cross-shoulder roll.

6/21/83, Doubts and a Dream

Dear Joey,

I am glad to be out every night. I like the night sky, picking out constellations or shooting stars – some so bright and wonderful as to be unbelievable. I saw a gold one, I swear it was gold colored; it went for way – way more than half way across the sky. It was big as a pencil's eraser. Although he had not seen it; he was out getting some wood; he did not doubt me. He thought, as I had, its size and color were both good omens. Apropos of nothing, I blurted out, "Is the only real reason you don't like me calling you Chief because I am not related to you by blood." He looked at me; and his facial expressions changed with each of the several considerations, which crossed his mind, if his face were any clue. He stopped stared and he began to say something, twice but ultimately he didn't. It was a test of Joey's and he said the Chief passed it with flying-colors. I do not know what it meant and, of course, Joey will not say.

I think we had another good omen. After we got the camp set for the night we watched the clouds to see if anything was up. He had told me the clouds brought news, usually of the weather. He said it looked good for travel before he went off to get busy with something or other as I sat watching the colors change; it was exactly like watching an ordinary fire. A couple of clouds sort of crisscrossed each other, became partly overlaid partly fitting together like puzzle pieces meeting. Curious, I watched. There came a moment when they made a perfect, and I mean to tell you, perfect, image of a horse doing a canter pace. It was so real I gasped. I went into myself and got Joey to look at it. He was amazed too. I did not take my eyes off as I called to my friend wondering what he would make of it. Oddly, he pretended not to notice what I was talking about. Anyway, the horse in the sky lasted the better part of a minute; I could see its flowing mane, gold in the fading sunlight; the body was red-brown and its tail tapered into midnight. There was a hint of something mysterious in the glaring white of its eyes. I wanted a camera more than anything in the world! When it faded with the sunlight, dissolving into other clouds, I was saddened as its remains were lost in the darkening sky. I asked him what it meant, or would mean. I noticed had gotten darned quiet, even in his eyes. He did not tell me a story that night either; we silently fell asleep in our respective places.

After some long while I heard him moving around, without moving I whispered, "What's the matter?"

"Everything or nothing, you should know that by now Wind Foot." I did not like this sudden new name for me. I must have had a look on my face because he looked at me laughing, "Oh, you can wriggle all you want to on that hook. It is just like the worm to squirm when bigger things make smaller things suffer." As I was thinking to rejoin with "and visa versa" he added, "If I am a chief, as you say; that's one of the decisions I can make." I did not know what to say, worse, Joey said he was right. I was uncomfortable but I couldn't very well argue with both of them at the same time.

"Well, why are you up, anyway?" I could see he was tending a very small fire made wholly of coals. It made almost no smoke. He was alternately blowing on it or fanning it carefully. I could see the few sparks gently rise and blink out above it. The slight breeze brought me sweet pine incense though it was richly blended. The last time we had been near pine was a number of days ago. He tossed dried leaves onto the coals and a scent came to me, which had me thinking of spaghetti – and my mom. I was thinking about her as I looked at him when he placed his face down close to the coals softly blowing. His whole face took up a ruddy glow. It was not much to go by still it struck me as never before how lined his face was, how old, craggy.

For a moment, I was horrified, wildly imagining I'd rather be at home with my mom dealing with the comparatively simple problems of Vince than be out here with no place to go, being hunted while depending on a stranger. I was looking at him with fear as my heart pounded. I had a hard time breathing softly. I did not want him to know what I was feeling or thinking. He was mumbling in his language – this was the last straw. I was caught in something I did not understand.

It was dark. As I looked around furtively, it seemed, in the faint bloody light, there were cast up tall lanky shadows of things dancing just out of sight. I slowly unzipped my bag making absolutely no noise. I'd have to leave everything here when I ran for it. I thought of my mom, who was waiting for me to come home, how Vince had become a better person. Surely another try was worth it. Why did I leave in the first place? Terrified of moving, I was deeply exhausted and fuzzy headed I could not muster the will to move; yet I could not sleep. I saw him and our camp at the same time as I saw my old kitchen, backyard or some long ago beach on a bright day or my hands working in wet sand, a toddler's hands they were. Memories flew past my imagination's eye as if pages in a flipbook. If I fixed on some common memory, it would morph into a brief high-speed film. With those far more vivid, super charged memories, dripping with emotional content, going by torturously slow as I was wrung with despair, anger, happiness or melancholy. I was wet with sweat and fever. I could hardly see for the welling tears blurring my sight. He was involved with this. I felt dizzy or disordered and disoriented. I did not know what to think.

It was as if I was floating, comfortable. I couldn't bother even thinking of moving. I was getting rest. I heard Wind whisper, "Rest is best." I exhaled. All the pent up tension left my body. I began to breathe slowly and deeply for some long time. I noticed he was adding bits of this and that to the fire as odd scents came and went. With he sound of each breath I imagined the ocean with its sequential waves rushing up onto a broad sandy shore. I was relaxing down to my bones. I believed I could speak but did not know what I'd say. Worries slipped off. I began to feel light, as if in an elevator falling gently. Soon it was as if I was tethered while set afloat upon an unseen tide, which swayed me as it quietly swirled around past on its way out. I felt the rise and fall of slight waves as they softly, slowly rolled underneath. I did not care if I did not know what it was which went past or under me. It was of no matter to my mind. Sleep was dark profound and delicious!

When I woke, I was on a deserted ocean beach. The sun was bright and the air fresh. I walked down to the water's edge, kicked off my shoes and waited as a wave came in, rushing up to splash over my toes, feet and then swirled around my ankles. The water was cool and refreshing, my whole body tingled with life. I looked seaward. The sparkling ocean was vibrant, windswept and calm. I knew I had been worried about something though I could not recall what.

The beach was deserted. To the left was a lighthouse on an outcropping of rock. Sand dunes ran along behind along the coast as far as I could see. I had been here before, a long time ago. Some vague memory vanished before I could see it. I heard a distant voice.

I turned to look. There was a large yellow and white beach umbrella. It belonged to mom and dad; I remembered it as soon as I saw it. It was from the good old days. There would be a small crib underneath it. This place was the first thing I could ever recall from when my real dad was alive. Off in the far distance a couple watched their toddler play in the sand. It was I. Vince did not exist yet and the best of everything in my early life lay ahead.

Could I go talk to them? Maybe I'd walk by at a distance. I could hear their laughter as well as the radio they left behind quietly playing light jazz. A wind soughed softly pushing me back; was it a hint? Hesitant at first, then tentatively I went over to the umbrella and, looking over its top, saw my crib. There was some mail set in a pile. Before going closer, I looked to see them. They had sat down to play with me in the wet sand, making a castle I'd guess. The envelopes had mom's name on some; dad's was on others.

I stood there crying softly. When I looked to them again, a mist or fog had obscured them all. I waited. I wondered how they could leave the radio, her patent leather purse, picnic things, precious blanket, and the umbrella – trusting no one would steal any of them. I walked a ways off to sit down. I wanted to protect their things and to see them close up when they came back – not that I knew what I'd say. Could I tell them I was their child somehow all grown up? I wanted to see mom and dad in love, young and beautiful.

A fog bank formed up a bit beyond the lighthouse. As I sat there, it gathered up. When the breeze shifted the fog came on quickly, thin at first, it grew thicker with each heartbeat. It became cooler too. I walked to the water's edge again and looked back at this setting; the lighthouse was lost in the fog as was most of the coast, even the ocean was quiet. I watched as the farther dunes were hidden from view. The fog drew in close. I went back to the umbrella feeling certain they must come back any moment. The fog was thick, the sky gone. I could see a couple dozen feet about me. Soon my world was reduced to the umbrella, the remains of a picnic as the seaward portion of the beach, swept over now and again by a thin wash, before it retreated with an uncanny silence. The cloying mist thickened about me and soon pretty much everything out more than a few steps away from me was lost.

When the radio went, it was as if someone ran off with it. I had kept it tuned, glad for its music when the ocean was no longer heard. I ran after it, screaming for my dad, for anyone, for help! I had not gone far when a flow ice-cold air brought me up. Fearful, I stood stock still, until, reconsidering the value of the umbrella, I turned to look where I recalled it should be. It was out of sight. Panicked I might have lost it as well as the chance to meet my parents, I began to circle, as best I might though I could barely see my outstretched hands.

The beneath my feet grew hazy with fog. I stumbled over the picnic basket before I saw it then I got a hold on the blanket and crouched down. Soon I could soon see neither. Crawling, I found the umbrella's handle and then the crib, which had once held me so safely. The fog became a brighter and brighter kind of gray; I was snow blind and cried calling for mom and dad. I held onto the crib and wrapped myself in the small blanket I knew had to have been mine. I grew exhausted and fell asleep.

When I awoke, the beach was as barren as it was sunny. The lighthouse was gone too; this was not the same beach. I did not know what to make of it. I was curious however. Clambering up the dunes, I found there were no roads or buildings for that matter. I walked back down to the ocean for a washing swim. Oddly, as I approached, the tide began to run out. When I happened to stop, it did to and when I moved toward it again, again it went back. I tried a run but it receded all the faster and when I stopped again, the water did too.

For hours, I walked along the widest beach imaginable. The sun hovered warm in the clearest sky I ever saw. I kept looking at the sea as I walked. After a time, I whispered to it as if it were the wind. I sent a kiss in its direction. A moment later, I saw something on the horizon maybe a shadow. As it grew I saw it was moving my way. It was a large wave rising up impressively even though it was still far off. By the time I heard its roar, I had been running toward the dunes full tilt for some long seeming time.

I was still far from the dry sand not to mention the hills beyond. I could not swim and feared drowning. The water was directly behind yet I was tiring, barely able to jog. I was suddenly very terribly hungry; my stomach cramped up hard and I stumbled. I rose only to fall again as I contracted with horrific cramping pains. I was obsessed with recalling not only what I had eaten last but when, no matter my immanent danger. My feet clumped up with mud. I thought of the Chief, Wind and Joey. The water rose quickly around me. I started to swim. Sloshing waves dunked me down almost as often as I tried for air. I took in water and began coughing and choking. A huge wave put me under. In the darkness I could not figure which way was up. It got icy cold. I was gone.

I coughed violently and was shaking uncontrollably as I opened my eyes, yelling until I saw I was back in the real world. There was a glow to the east as a silent dawn crept onto the hilltops around me. Birds graced the sky with songs. Several near by were swooping about to nab insects. I heard nestlings call. There was a nearby stream. I could smell the water in the air before I heard it.

I went toward the sound. He was fishing. There was a second pole set up. Without a word, we fished. We did not catch a thing. Somehow, a lot did happen between us even though I'm unable to explain it. I mean, after that dream, I knew I was awake to every sound and nuanced gesture he made. We talked, without words, of many things.

Joey is gone or I know he was me. I know I'm special the way I always believed he was. Wind is takes to me differently – it won't talk or do anything I want, whenever I want, like bring papers or scatter a trail. I've to think about this more because it seems weird. We made 50 miles, easy.

6/25/83

Dear Joey,

Today we went through hills above a small town. We've been making good time ever since the night of the dream. We don't talk much or rather I don't. He may when we pass a mountain or valley he knows something about. Sometimes, it's about a plant I'll need to know or a track of some little being, that's what he calls animals, little beings. He says that's what they are. He says considering them as such makes it harder to kill them foolishly. He thinks the little beings are going to get together one day to tell men, Indians included, how to live in harmony with them; I can't wait for such a day, it'll be great. I can imagine squirrels, bats, deer, and fish going on strike or raising a ruckus to mess things up until we humans come around to a new way of living. We'd have to listen to the earth and its living carpet then but then again we're clueless.

I got him to laugh, when I told him a story Vince liked to tell about a place called Warm Springs. The town once made a statue honoring those who had died in the Philippine War and, of course WW1 and so forth. The town fathers placed the impressive statue atop a large boulder in town's main intersection where seven different roads came to a nexus. The idea being, everyone would see it no matter which road was used. When cars came along, they strung the intersection with an array of signal lights meant to direct traffic about the statue and its circle. Problem was the statue blocked the view of at least two of the other streets no matter which one you used on your approach. This arrangement resulted in accidents over the years. As the deaths mounted slowly, they rearranged the lights, restricted traffic or made some streets one-way. However, drivers still used their horn along with naked luck as the main strategies to successfully navigate the intersection – the city never did give up rearranging signals or lights. Well, as Vince told it, what happened was, eventually, they moved the thing but it wasn't until the number of people who had died on the monument exceeded the number of names engraved into the stone. Vince had said it "goes to show that pain makes progress." My friend laughed heartily. The rest of the day chuckled every now and then shaking his head. I guess he agrees with Vince as I did.

We're good at avoiding people as we go along but, if we do meet other hikers, we've a cover story, which is embellished as we go. We steer clear of drifters not wanting to borrow any kind of trouble.

We've clear skies for the most part, sometimes morning fog or mist but no rain. We keep to the near the ridges and almost never go into towns. I like the smell of the wind up here; it's clean, brisk like a good day at the beach. Many of the valleys we pass have their bottomland quilted with small family farms. We're not surprised at how the more rural a place, the better we feel about going down for odds and ends. People of hamlets assume what we tell them is true; that we're hikers passing by on the long backcountry trail. He tells them he's a retired park ranger while I'm his step-nephew. I can look years older, he taught me how. People accept I am 18, what with being a bit weather worn, and way I dress and act, even if I seem a bit short.

Sometimes we get nice conversations with good-hearted people also trekking along. It's right plain comforting when we share ideas or knowledge in an easy flowing exchange where a nod or gesture can be worth a thousand words. It's all a part of our ancient past and its simplicity and justice. Sometimes I chirp right up about the plants right around us – or those they'll see along the trail.

Once we talked with a man, who was in his eighties, about what grows where or when, how to pickle or prepare certain kinds of roots, and about herbs and medicinal flowers. We got into swapping tales. His wife made a kind offer to break bread. To my surprise we quickly said, "sure." With a knowing glance, we each agreed they'd probably know food. They sure did. We were all smiles by the time we were done. The man sent us off with a prayer as he waved farewell for some time. We had told so many stories and laughed so hard, especially concerning the shortcomings of the kind of people who would starve right next to greens or throw money away expensive condiments, which were growing right in their yard – or in the open spaces around where they live. "Too much TV" I'd said "and idle entertainment, drives them all batty," which got everyone laughing. Grandpa Davis, that was his title, said, to me, "You sound like my father and isn't that a fine thing for a kid of today." When they all nodded in silence and smiled my way, it was one of the best moments of my life; I understood what 'heartwarming' meant.

On our way back into the hills, I lamented. I knew we shouldn't have stayed for any time. How could we? By accepting an invitation, we knew was right for many reasons, we not only risked being seen but put a couple of dear innocents in danger. My friend agreed which is why he had declined their kind offer for staying for dinner with a couple of friends. With a gesture and a glance, I comprehended his train of thought, we would want desert, which meant even more rich talk and we'd grow confident, comfortable then come to see no problem with staying overnight. This would mean, in turn, breakfast. There would be the risk of leaving during daylight when there was no way of telling if anyone might see us as a group. A single emphatic gesture on my part spoke of how angry I was at having to live with such pervasive fear. It was no matter how well placed our trust was, we had to leave off. As we left we were burdened by a real worry for our one-time hosts. We feared that the same cold, silent trackers, who would never leave off seeking our trail, might now show up on their doorstep. I did not sleep very well. I saw anguish and flames in my dreams. He slept poorly too.

We broke camp early next morning to ascend the hills overlooking their valley. We could still see their store on the crossroads; we looked on until the sun came up and we stretched in its warmth before turning away.

New days forever refreshing, that's what it feels like. I'm getting stronger all the time. We can make 50 to 60 miles in a day or more if we push it; I've learned to walk. Now it may sound funny – but you have to learn how to walk out here. One false step can lead to pain or crippling death, if you're in wrong circumstances. You've got to watch every footfall, place your feet each step of the way, using the ground's slightest contour to help. There are always little niches to gain a toehold or placements worthy of consideration for nearly every step. It is very efficient. Every time I place my foot, I measure how to save energy. Even when we're in town, we walk soft which means not making a whisper, no jiggling of some doodad on your pack, in fact, there shouldn't be doodads. In order to bring this home

to me, he once hung several paper clips from strings attached to
my pack and jacket. I had to walk with care so he wouldn't hear
them tapping as he went along silently beside me. I discovered
all those leg muscles one doesn't use much – though if you work
with them, you don't get nearly as tired. We walk soft. I've not
used any money for a long time. I've over 6,000 dollars so
"howzaboutdemappeln" as my dad used to say.

6/27/83

Dear Joey,

I awoke last night; he was singing. It was still; the air
was unusually warm. He'd a small bed of coals and some small
items, which gave off incense. I looked at him with a question
on my face; this caught his eye. He stopped, glanced my way. I
understood he'd tell me when he was done. After a short while,
he stopped and turned to face me to see if I was awake. I was,
barely so. I stretched and sat up; he translated the song:

> **I am touched**
> **many have been before me**
> **on this trail**
> **I see what they have left**
> **long have I come**
> **with company**
> **such as this**
> **the wheel marks**
> **remnants of cargo**
>
> **the day bows**
> **above thought**
> **spans time**
> **I pass fields**
> **it is so clear**

the straw matting
laying out in the sun
a barking dog
a farmhouse window
its
white curtain
hangs out
tells the wind   that
tells my face
and these gentle leaves
flourish color
rich in death
these do not scorn their wisdom
accepting their given work
they ply no reason
from being
what they are
their will
or virtue
they rustle in the wind
burn quickly in fire
and are the strength of these woods
they
do not beg
in life
for its
taste
simply
is too sweet

I didn't mean to laugh as I did. He looked hurt so I told him songs are supposed to rhyme, have some kind of rhythm and have a clear, simple meaning. I asked what kind of song it was anyway. He remained crouched over the tiny glow. He stared at me as if at a puzzle. I guessed it was his kind of song; not the old songs of his people even, just what he creates as he goes along his way. He shrugged – he thought it was better than anything I could do. I shrugged, meaning I'm no singer, he said, "So you should learn." He sang another:

All there is

All there is   the color of it
tiny   hint: moss
a single blade of grass
its shadow across their commune
at this exact time of day

the commune lives
on a fragment
of curled earth
(the earthworm at work)
soft and green
they take in the sun
letting air
in and out
in and out
they continue
on a curdle of earth
In the shadow blade of grass
to weave

Well, at least I could picture one well enough. I liked better than the first one. I yawned again as did he – agreeing I should sleep since we had a long day tomorrow. I looked at him as quizzically as if to say – what about you; don't you have to sleep? His eyes steady upon mine – he didn't need to and that was all there was to it. Soon I was out like a light, as my mom used to say.

We made 55 miles by mid afternoon. Having been let to lead, I'd gotten a hard tempo going. I smiled to myself as I set a challenging pace. We were heading for a mountain. It took longer than we'd thought. However, by the time we were beginning to ascend, some ominous clouds overshadowed it. I felt we'd have a hard time finding a good site on the steep incline we were ascending. When we broke for a late lunch, we glanced about, looked at each other and shrugged at the same time – we agreed: before the first irritating or tentative sprinkling of the soon to be borne storm tapped us we had to have our site picked out. I sniffed to suggest we find something quick – and lunch, such as it was, some dried fish, fruit, sprouts, water with nearby greens, was over.

The mountain was not tall as mountains go. It was good we found only animal trails; it meant a much smaller chance of running into anyone. He had chosen our approach when we surveyed the mountain earlier – so we had him to thank for the tough going through rough brush over rocky, uneven ground, all of which made for careful going. I was surprised however at the ground cover's marvelous variety of small plants with their tiny flowers. As the afternoon got late, the upper air was moving and clouds' shadows began to flow across the peak. We were soon walking amid chilling mists, which had my outer layers grow damp.

As daylight faded, I headed for a low pair of trees, which, set against an outcrop of rock provided a nice hideaway, shelter from the wind, and more. I didn't consult him but assumed, since he followed, he had accepted my judgment. It was not as level as I hoped though it would serve. By the time we made fast our tenting material it was drizzling. I stood looking down slope; I heard voices, soft, at distance from the north – probably moving away. I tracked the sound until I was sure that whoever it was wouldn't be crossing our trail. He nodded; I smiled, in our kind of silence we guessed some unlucky hikers were heading back toward the last town. I smiled – I hoped they were well prepared for the storm; he nodded – yes, it was a long way back to the trailhead.

I began to teach him how to play checkers. I beat him six straight but last game was touch and go all the way to the end; he smiled.

6/30/63

Dear Joey,

It was wonderful this morning; birds had already taken to the air. Their fleet songs were my first hints of the real world. I slept under the blanket I had suspended over a single strand of rope, which I'd tied between two trees and I tucked both sides of it under me. The meadow was humming with all the little beings that work their lives away in, under or above the verge. I listened for a time. It was already warm by the time I made some noise. He was still asleep which was most unusual as he's the one who rouses first, likes to breathe the fire back into flame while I get good water, if we're luxuriating, that is. I almost wanted to chide him for being a sleepy worm, the kind an early bird gets. I got up, turned out the coals, blew them into glowing while carefully added a few small twigs and sticks. I soon had my "cup of fire" going nicely. I heard him sniff once or twice before he began to stir.

He seemed pleased as he slowly rousted himself and ambled over. He looked over the pot with its small setting, two cups, a plastic bag containing honey and a spoon all set upon my outspread and most colorful handkerchief. He grunted, sat down pouring tea as I turned to finish packing up. I was proud no hint of disapproval had come, for surely I'd have heard something if anything was amiss. I was sure the fire had been made right, hardly a whiff of smoke graced the air for I had banked it so well I didn't need match – the tinder caught up easily. We had tea in silence. I was clearly pleased with myself. He had neither said nor indicated anything. He licked his lips indicating so tea was good, took in a deep breath before letting it out sighing – he'd slept exceptionally well and was glad for it. He tapped his shoe – I knew there were some hard walks ahead of us. He grimaced, as he looked skyward before nodding. I guessed, to avoid some of the bad weather we might get in the mountains between here and Arizona, we'd have to make a good pace from now on. Arizona, or rather our destination inside it, was still hundreds of miles away.

I hummed a bit of a folk song and stopped; I wanted him to sing and without missing a beat he did:

Morning Song:

exhausted
fallen away
the lime blossoms give all they can
to be with us   so
these are for you
from seventh garden   smell
these   special limes
fresh from the trees
blessed by the birds
whose fleet songs
taper this summer's eve
come walk with me here
where Venus rises over the hills
unfolding
in the heavens
dawn's gossamer
she'll embroider each flower and blade
with a morning song
and within
each drop of dew   gleam

I liked that one a lot. I had nodded to him so he repeated a few times until I was able to sing along. It had a simple quality. One did not have to have a good voice to sing it; in such a way, it was like a folk song – the tune seemed similar.

I looked out over the valley, which yawned out behind us trying to trace the route we'd come by. I could not see a particular rock formation I had wanted to use as marker. As I looked for another landmark, I saw five persons about as many miles behind us. I could hear them when Wind brought the sound along. From it I could tell they pushing their pace but, thankfully, they were proceeding on a course that angled away from ours. I turned to him with a nod as I raised my brows; he looked their way and gestured to hunker down. He did not want to move until he had watched them for nearly twenty minutes. I was surprised; he usually made up his mind much more quickly about those who pass us by so closely. I was impatient to leave. I cautiously put the fire away banking it first to avoid tell tale signs. Both it and sleeping in had been luxuries we, it seems, could still not afford. Had we been on our way a couple of hours ago, we'd not be anywhere near them or they us. I heard him mutter, "Good breakfast; nice sleep ... "

Oh, I got it, all right. Those were nice, however, putting ourselves at risk was not. His ensuing silence however told me there was no need to apologize especially after it was clear they weren't closing. We decamped. Wind did its bit to sweep up, just in case. The last we saw they were still going off at an angle. We could only speculate as to whether they were innocent or not but we did not think they'd catch our trail. We changed course keeping to rocky ground and kept to cover as we could.

All day no one else came as close as those five. We made great progress, sixty miles even with a long lunch rest and setting up camp early. I made dinner again. He laughed when, after I had done everything perfectly, as far as far as I could tell, I lost most of the tea, spilling it onto the fire. Not only did I nearly put it out but sent up as nice a plume of steam as you might like. We laughed so hard we cried. It was funny despite the possibility of giving away our position. We changed out, decamped, and did another 10 miles before dropping back on a course nearly parallel to way we'd come. We doglegged a few times to confuse any would be follower before stopping to sleep. We kept watches. When he noticed my silence, I finally hit myself in the head – I was that angry. He joked it off saying, "It was all right, everyone makes a mistake; that's how life goes on and on; and besides, it makes things interesting – it's why pencils have erasers."

Apparently to get my mind off the subject he began telling a story. He and his brother, it seems, were once interested in the same girl though she ultimately went off with someone else. The long tale revealed that not only was the guy someone they both disliked; it was also he, as they later found out, who set them up not only to fight each other but in so doing used them to demonstrate his qualities to the woman. As he told it, this guy arranged matters so they "put up dukes" with gusto and foul oaths just as he "happened" by. Then, as he heroically tried to talk sense to them both and was being treated very roughly for it, the woman in question also "just happened by." She, in bearing witness to the "happy scene," saw the two brothers in very poor light while the jerk's faux "heroics" put him in good with her. What with his comparatively smooth talk and her graceful sympathies, he walked off with her – right under their very big bruised noses.

My friend continued saying not only was he pained by the blows received and given but there was a deep, nay exquisite, humiliation to boot. He was not able to easily best his brother and he had been out witted by some one, who was generally disliked and looked down upon. His brother also saw him as a fool and, of course, they both lost the girl. These events became memories, which sharpened each other until the insult was worked into a grievous injury.

Typical of how he tells stories, after about a half an hour, the tale had only started. It gradually meandered onward through the years. Soon after their fight they attempted to revenge themselves during a harvest festival. They siphoned gasoline from the guy's car after he'd taken her to a lover's lane so he brought the young lady home far later than he should have. This, in turn, caused some trouble with the girl's father. When dad took the young man home, he not only found the guy's car with a half a tank of gas in it but it started on the first try. Matters got worse, when the father chased the boy into his house and, after breaking into the boy's room, he saw some of the girl's clothes draped across his bed. However, if breaking up the lovely couple was the aim of their prank, it was not to be. Neither of them figured there'd be a forced a marriage, nearly on the spot. Then, although the marriage did not last long, there were kids as well as a great deal of grief for the woman, the man with a few further misadventures between her, my friend, and his brother. In sum, there was more than enough unhappiness to go around and no one missed their ample servings. When I looked at him as if to ask, what is the point, he shrugged indicating that he'd forgotten and laughed.

That night we set up a blind so we could play checkers by candlelight, a luxury we felt we could afford after having come so long a way. Although he lost the first three, those were followed by three draws before he won the last game.

7/1/83

Dear Joey,

The overnight rain wasn't too bad; I liked the sound on my tent/blanket. The air was fresh, beautiful. I dreamt of being an eagle flying amid clouds high above them all with only the sun above me. As far as I could see, towards the end, there was nothing save bright white clouds below a blue sky. I went swooping down yet stayed above the clouds. I laughed, nearly loosing control. When I came in for a landing I flew over an encampment of men, I knew who and what they were.

So, we both woke, jumped up, as we packed we gobbled some dry food and guzzled water to get on our way as fast as possible. For the first time in a long time, as I happened to be sitting still, Wind came to me and spoke:

"Be still if you will. There are those who draw near. They work out of fear. They guide those who will not fail. These are they who are on your trail."

I was startled, looked over to my friend, winked and tossed my head back – we're being followed.

He shrugged, sighed and blinked – so what else is new, we've done it before we have to do it again, let's get a move on buddy. Tapping my heart – I'd felt it. He gave a thumbs up – he was sure. We did not slack a motion, but hurried taking all the slight shortcuts. Since I was done before him, I began to clean traces when Wind came up and took care of it. My friend looked at me, the sky, and his eyes were full of questions yet there was no time.

We tied string to a heavy stick and, as we walked, every once in a while, when we were going over barren rock, we'd throw the thing off to one side or the other and drag it back creating false leads intended to slow trackers; it was my idea – from a movie. He did some swiping himself, as we went along. Wind puffed in a bit every once in a while. I mentally browsed the things Joey had memorized about throwing off a tracker. The simplest was to be expert at taking steps and moving around rather than brushing aside plants but it was slower. This worried us. When I nearly fell, my friend stopped, looked me square in the eye – was I was all right. I gestured this way and that – I couldn't keep my mind on the trip. "Well, you'd better learn quick or we're gonna have company. Are you any good with what passes for the law out here?"

"No." I worried that the Wind had been "iffy" of late, sometimes around, sometimes not. I'd been worried about this as

I tried to make use of everything I knew. It was hard to keep track of everything.

He jerked his head toward the east, frowned at me and pointed to his feet – I'm going to set a heavy pace eastward; I hope your feet are ready. I gave him a long blink – let's just get going and quite all the bellyaching. I didn't tire; I was amazed at the miles we covered, 110. We still felt some party was near enough to notice, though these were not the ones we'd dusted for they were coming from a different direction than before. I figured that we'd left Nevada far behind.

7/2/83

Dear Joey,

He told me his long ago people came from the far north at one time before settling in Arizona. Part of his family still owns land there. He figures I could stay as long as I want. I won't have to worry living in peace.

I looked forward to meeting his family. We couldn't go into a town to call ahead. It would be insanely inconvenient not to mention stupidly dangerous; we'd stand out like neon cowboys on fishing boat. I believed him when he said all we had to do was show up and say hello. We were managing well with what we gathered or the occasional bit of game. Now he was the one who was surprised when I pointed out plants, recited their stories or details about them if not the means to prepare them as food. Joey, I mean, I had done a remarkable job with those books and his stories.

We had a scent of trouble today. My friend had gone to scout around, while I got grub together. When he got back, he signed he'd seen a wilderness ranger watering his horse at a small spring. He crept up on the man then followed him. It was why he was away so long. He hadn't seen the guy use a radio. Still, when I told him that Wind hadn't seen anyone else for miles and miles, he was not assured and seemed worried. Then I worried and we both were a bit on edge, rattled I'd say.

We moved on after nightfall. We got some miles away and saw, behind us, set of thunderheads gathering with a few flickers of lightning beneath them. As he looked back I chuckled – good luck to those trying to find a trail, if we'd left any, it would be lost in the ensuing confusion. He nodded but with a slight grimace – he doubted it would be enough.

We both knew luck wasn't enough; we kept to our routines. The trackers, whomever they were, had radios, networks of minions who could be called to take up positions ahead of us, send scouts snooping around or monitor us from the sky. Since we could never know whether we were free of them, we had to assume we weren't.

We're still a few days away from "being close" as he calls it. It meant another week or more of stealthy going. I wasn't concerned. In my mind, I was already there. I could see it. In my dreams I saw them waiting on us and looking at the moon even as I did in my dreams.

7/3/83

Dear Joey,

It was a new morning with very clean refreshing air. You could smell the dew. The little I heard let me know he was already up, had the tea set to steep, and had found some greens. We got going.

Near around noon, we topped a ridge. We saw an open desert valley, probably about 60 miles wide with one thin road running its length. He promptly sat, surveying – meaning we'd be visible for miles and miles. I sighed – there were the other problems too. I touched my palm where lines crossed – there was stuff on the map, gave a faux salute – there was a military base in the area, and I licked my lips, it was going to be very hot out there. He shook his head and nodded toward the other side and shrugged – we had to assume we were pressed, had no choice but to go, and quickly. He stared into north and then to south even longer, and finally shrugged meaning – to go around the thing would mean a couple days of real hotfooting. I nodded in reply – on the other side were some nice mountains. I recollected that he'd said his brother knew them, which meant we were "a little close." He looked at me and we silently planned it out. We'd best cross at night, cover ourselves during the day, and finish crossing next night. That's what we did. By the time it began to get light, we were close to the road. We dug shallows, covered up with a tarp and Wind softly blew over a slight covering of sand.

7/3/83 – 7/4/83

Dear Joey,

We're on the other side of the valley tonight. The sun is going down on what became a day of rest, because, almost right off, we caught a ride from some farm workers "going our way." They slowed down to take a look at us before offering us a chance to work or a ride along. One of them knew my friend a little-bit as they put it and I felt rush of optimism choosing to believe our fortunes were improving. We told a few stories meant to leave false trails, should anyone talk to he farm workers later on. When the truck stopped at a small roadside building an office manager came out to get names and check fitness. He asked everyone questions. I was puzzled but my friend handled it. After learning the big boss man's name my friend suddenly changed tack to say he had shoulder trouble and couldn't do the work being. I kept mum.

As we started on our way, he rolled his eyes—he'd known the big boss and figured we'd been walking into trouble. Second, not an hour later, we got a ride into the hills in the back of an old man's pickup. He was a happy old codger and as glad to talk as we were to get a second ride. He wouldn't take anything for helping us so we left a chunk of change in one of his boxes where he'd find it as soon as he unloaded. He invited us for dinner. When we declined, it looked as though we'd hurt his feelings. We couldn't help it; we'd learned our lesson. The faster we traveled the better able we were to avoid trouble. Also, the less he knew about us, the better, for him!

We were glad to be across the valley. It had been I who'd argued for risking a hitch with my thumb to give old Lady Luck a whirl for a change. Wind found no one near us. I could see nothing through the ring. The random element had clearly worked in our favor.

We were sitting around the fire. I looked into the small flames as he was whittling a stick. The crickets were singing and the sky was clear. It was a warm night and we were close to being happy. This was what life should be like. All I want to do is have a healthy change to figure out what I want to do with my life. Is that too much to ask?

7/4/83

Dear Joey,

When I woke up, I began to make breakfast. It was my turn. I went about my business. When he got up what he did was bizarre or weird, never saw the like. Curious, I had to ask him what he was doing.

"I am grinding this salt into powder," he replied.

"So it is salt, and you are grinding it. Why here, why now and, uh, why at all?" I had not recalled him picking anything like that up. Also I noticed it was mostly pink it was vari-colored.

"We will need it."

"Well, it looks like you have about 10 or more pounds of it. I don't think we will need that much, even in a year."

"This is not for seasoning," he added.

"Well, what is it for then?"

"Traveling, this is sea salt, the blood of all life is here. We will need it for traveling," he spoke as if to provide an explanation but, as it did not explain, I let it go. I tended the fire and made a soup from dried greens, meat and roots. It was looking very good. I called him when it was ready. I sat with him in silence as we ate. We had some real nice apricots we'd picked up and dried over the last week.

I had watched him as he ground up all of the salt, rolled it into a cone of newspaper. He tore off its tip to make a pour spout, which he folded and tucked under. I said nothing.

We made ready for travel. Wind whipped in behind us to clear any traces. I was surprised when my friend actually said thank you, to Wind I mean, it was a first for him. Yet, again, I kept my silence. I was going to keep it until he noticed. I was going to ask about the salt but only if he spoke first. He did not.

We only made about 45 miles. The steep climbing and temperature were rough on us both. We are doing double duty as we went doing all we could to cover our trail as if we knew we were tracked even if at distance.

Oh, yes, he has not told me yet.

7/10/83, The Implacable Foes

Dear Joey,

I couldn't sleep well. I dreamt of some vague shadowy man, or something, which would not go away, even when I used the ring and Wind. I couldn't find the Chief. I wanted to be sure he was safe and near by.

I woke to his singing and saw he had a real cooking fire going, smoke and all. Our best food had been set out. He was using nearly all of our cooking stuff. He was preparing a feast.

I gestured – what's the occasion?

He looked around nodding first in one direction, and in a couple more – we were surrounded. The way he signed it however, was as if to say we needed to be ready for our guests – since we have considerable company.

I looked. I saw nothing. I waited alert. I heard sounds from a couple locations. A scent drifted in from yet another. Yup, more than three groups. He signed for an owl, a rabbit, and a mountain lion – they had good eyes, were fast, quiet, could hear, and were deadly.

How could we've been followed! We'd been careful and Wind had done its part. I was suddenly afraid. A sinking feeling took hold in my gut. I felt all the stage fright one could feel. I almost felt dizzy. I was angry. I wanted to fight them, whomever they were, wherever they were.

I took out my ring, set myself up, and got still to whisper for Wind. I was going to press it into service. I was getting the first whispers at my ear when I heard him stand up, walk over to where I was. He stood there a moment, pushed me off balance, I gestured – hey, why did you do that?

He made a sweeping skyward motion – he didn't want me to use the Wind. He pointed to where he believed the men to be and signed – it would be exactly what they'd want. If I let them see it again they'd know, more than ever, what it was they were trailing. Another set of signs – he believed they'd never give up and then maybe his family couldn't even hide me. He thought we'd be hounded forever. Tapping his head – he wondered if I grokked such a thing yet.

I pointed to my eyes, the sky, and the fire then made a sweeping gesture – they had eyes in the sky and could spot a campfire easily, especially way out here. He made another set of gestures – the people on the lookout for us had the unwitting help of many. I shrugged, pointed all around and doffed my hat, meaning – it didn't matter where we went.

He looked at me, sadly, and finished saying, "I don't want them to know such a power exists. They'll abuse it as sure as they've abused everything else under the sun."

"Of whom do you speak?" I signed.

"In a long ago time there were wars between what we would call races now. Most all have no memory of it however family does. From them I know these wars have never ended and so the ones that are happening today are not at all what they seem to be or all about what everyone, even the leaders of the warring nations, believe them to be. There are levels of puppets, it seems." He was desperate, almost angry and spoke in a shouting whisper more harshly than I'd ever thought possible.

"So we're going to have a nice big breakfast, sit back to wait for the men in gray to come and take us away? Is such a thing our big plan?" I was angry, though more at my own confusion than what he'd said. He sighed as he looked at me sadly motioning me over to the fire.

"We have no worry. There is only one way to kill the story they must be weaving up in preparation for our capture and that means we have time. I plan to play it close. We must look as though we do not expect anything. That we feel safe and secure. Like I say, we have time."

"How long do you figure?"

"Being as some of them could run all the way here, they could have taken us at any time last night. It must be they're waiting for some honcho who wants to show and so claim to count coup."

I looked over the food spread out before me and my mouth watered. I made an inclusive gesture then pointed at my wrist – I might as well eat well now; I might not have any time later. It smelled so good. He'd made his special biscuits with honey raisins, the best.

We did eat well. We used up dried vegetables in a soup, the sprouts we had combined with some local vegetables. Some sweet onions were in the mix too. We topped it off with dried fruit I had steamed drizzled with more honey. We sat back and relaxed. Although I knew this was temporary, I did not let reality alter my good feelings. We didn't even bother to clean our mess kits or the campsite. I was thinking about how we would appear to be what were supposing to be, contented, secure campers with nothing to fear at all.

He began to sing to himself as he relaxed sitting with his back to a tree stump. His closed his eyes, was happy, and at ease for the first time since I'd met him. I too laid back. I looked into the sky as I listened. It seemed to be a short song, which repeated over and over. Later he gave me the translation:

**If all the leaves
on all the trees
were tongues
they could not say
the word
for all this love of all.**

It was the high afternoon when I awoke from a nap. He was still asleep; the campsite was a mess. I began cleaning up and mentally second guessing what we'd do for grub – not that we would want anything fancy or large however something was called for. He slumbered on as I got the site cleaned. I rattled of a couple of the pans to rouse him from his reverie. We finished the clean and were packed tight in about a half an hour. I took the opportunity to switch into some clean clothes.

It was a beautiful day. I was in a good mood until I caught sight of a movement along the ridge a few hundred yards off to the southwest. I was surprised that I'd forgotten our problematical friends hiding in the low rolling hills around us. I looked to him. He signed that he'd seen a bright reflection, which may have been light glancing off a pair of binoculars or some bit of metal, neither of these events were considered serious. We spent the better part of two hours watching a pair of ants nests fight over some bread we'd dropped as we argued over what we should do or not do about it. We got rather heated on the subject, raised our voices and hushed each other a few times. It got so bad we changed our minds out of frustration as well as spite. We laughed in the end when we noticed the bread had disappeared even as our argument reached the improbable heights of idiocy, which is to say politics and philosophy. Then came to see we'd done them wrong, inadvertently causing a dispute of monstrous proportions for when the bread was gone this only seemed to rouse further fury in the war. Ultimately, we placed more bread in areas closer to the two nests and the war drew to a close as the day waned.

All we had for dinner was some sweet tea and a stew made from our dried stores. We stayed around the fire long after the sunlight faded listening to the silence of dusk and the start up of nocturnal voices. We were waiting for our visit.

As the moon set he suddenly got to his feet. He had been asleep or dozing. He looked at me, pointed to his eyes – and then around – he wanted to see how or what they were doing.

I patted the earth – you don't want me to go with you; someone has to stay here to make it look good. I intended overtly to make a point, which I saw him recognize though all he did was nod and shrug his shoulders before going into his tent making a bit of a fuss about it. I sat tending the fire though I shifted position so my shadow covered the side of his tent. He was as quiet as fog when he moved out on the dark side of the tent into the further dark surround. Every once in a while, I spoke, as if in reply to him. I wrote in my diary. I was nervous. I let the fire settle down, intending to bank it.

I actually heard him coming back. Winded and stumbling, clearly in a panic, something was wrong. When he came out of my tent, I signed – I'm all ears.

"I've hurt two men. They were over the ridge where you saw movement. I moved on their campsite to investigate. I was quiet, as God is my sweet witness; I was quiet. I rendered them unconscious as quickly and as quietly as you please. I rooted around for anything handy after I couldn't find any ID, which of course told me a lot. I heard a couple voices coming my way. I couldn't get away without being seen. Knowing, also, I'd be seen quickly so I stood with my back to the fire as they approached, wearing one of their hats and coat. I asked them to halt, they did; I walked up to them, shining a light in their eyes. I put one of them down quickly though the other ducked and we fought it out – it got messy."

I gave the mortal sign with a twist – did you kill them?

He touched at his heard and signed ok – my heart reassures me I did not. He showed a fist and this touched his heart – I was fearfully angry. I was fighting for my life. Then a few other signs – I do know one thing; we must leave here. If we do it your way, it will force our hand. We will always be on the run. That's no life.

I shook my finger at him – so, what are we going to do?" I was puzzled. How were we to get out of this one? Maybe it was time to quit. Our talents could be used for good. Maybe we could have a good life doing good things for people. That wouldn't be so bad. We could be heroes.

Apropos of nothing, it seemed to me, he said, "Now is the time for the salt." He said this as if it was an explanation though, again, I did not understand. He had us gather up our stuff, and place it at a spot about 20 feet from the fire. We sat down in the dark with our gear in a pile about us. I looked at him expectantly. He was quiet, staring off, as my eyes adjusted to the darkness he mumbled a bit.

He motioned – hunker down; do not move. "I am going to use the salt," he said. Using a simple stick he drew a rough ellipse in the dirt enclosing our gear and us. He went around three times, pressing it hard into the same track as he murmured. Then, in silence, he laid the salt into the track. He sat back down and began swaying to the beat of the nearly inaudible song he whispered. I kept looking over to him having nothing else to do nor able to think for myself at this point. I was going with the flow, letting it all happen. I felt the breeze on the cool air while a few crickets marked their own kind of time.

He paused as if to listen he paused and ceased singing, looked at me and smiled.

My incredulous look spoke volumes, the gist of which was – and that's it?

His thumbs up – yup, that's it. Still with that silly look– and his wide grin, which only got wider. He added, "Now you know a great deal about me and my tribe. I only did this because I can trust you as a child may be trusted by its father."

I looked at him as he looked at me. I had never heard either of us use such a term openly either with each other or about each other. I trusted him. He was not my father; there were things about him I didn't like, on the other hand he was consistent, honest in dealing with me, and willing to listen. He respected me and allowed me to be who I was. He could admit it when he made a mistake. I remember Vince would never admit to a mistake. Even my mother would have a hard time admitting to an error. It was as if everyone in the whole world held it was a sin to be found wrong and worse yet to admit to it. It was a real taboo. We'd worked together and walked some hundreds of miles. I reached out to take his hand. My hand seemed so soft and small compared to his huge weathered specimen, which was surprisingly warm, comforting, and strong. I'd trust his hands with my life.

"Soon you will see great magic," he said, "soon."

"What will happen?" By that I meant, I was not at ease; what with the fact that there was now more than a hint of light in the sky and that we, and our gear, were, if anything, even more out in the open, not to mention those men being hurt, it all added up to the fact that our company would arrive any moment – and then what? What would we be able to do against them, especially if I am not to use Wind? When he did not answer me, I began to standup. As quick as lightening, he grabbed a hold on me and pulled me down to the ground.

"Don't stand up!" He was angry, but also fearful, for me. I didn't understand but when I tried to stand again, again he pulled me down.

"What is wrong with you," I demanded, "you aren't making sense. Those men can be here any minute; you want to sit and wait for what? Did they get to you? Are you working with them? Is this all some sort of trap?"

This proved too much for him. His attitude broke. He grabbed me forcefully by the shoulders in his two powerful hands digging in and it hurt, I thought of Vince and struggled with him.

But he held me fast. "Look at me," he said, "look at me and be quiet. They will not find us!"

"But we are out in the open. It's going to get light. How are we to hide?"

"We are hidden now, except for your voice. We are already hidden; they cannot find us no matter how hard they look. Look around you what do you see?"

At first, I could only look into his eyes; I was in a rage, thinking he was crazy. Then, as I calmed, I noticed it had gotten quiet; then, as they used to say in the old westerns, it was too quiet. There were no crickets, breeze, birds, or coyotes. I blinked my eyes to break his gaze. As I glanced around, it seemed to be getting darker instead of lighter, as it should have. "What's happening to the light?" I whispered, truly puzzled.

He released his grip, saying, "We are disguised from it, from them." He was calm as he watched me look about. I knew some kind of trick was going on. "Look at the sky now,"

I looked straight up. It was as if a night sky was swallowing up everything in sight and in a moment there was complete dark all around us. I couldn't see my hand in front of my face, although I felt the men nearby despite the fact it was quiet outside.

"What is this?" I whispered.

"This is the shelter of time. My people use it when we have no recourse. I didn't want to show you but had to. Your trust demanded it." Again, this answer did not make sense; I simply looked toward his voice waiting for him to continue.

"The salt is the key as is a song which must be sung; that's how you build it. To us on the inside, it gets dark because far, far less light enters." All I could hear was our breathing and his murmured words. He continued: "To those on the outside the shelter, it appears as a stone, a large boulder, either gray brown or some other mix of colors depending on the mix of minerals in the salt used to create the illusion, the time diffraction, or distortion. While it is forming sound is also blocked until it stabilizes that is. Then it becomes transparent to sound.

"What happens if I stand up?"

"It would pop as if it were a soap bubble, however if you're caught in it as it does so, you get cut in two.

"Can we get out?"

"Oh, sure, no problem at all, we huff and puff and blow a hole in the line of salt and the bubble gradually dissolves, after a moment or two but we must wait until they are gone."

"How will we know if we can't see them, or anything else outside of this thing?

"If it's dark outside we can look out by holding a light to the edge or, if it is daytime, we hold a mirror up to it." With that, he lit a lighter and, in the circle of its glow upon the otherwise invisible barrier, we could see outside. It was just past dawn. A number of men encircled our location although none was closer than twenty feet. We heard them talking. They were angry. He told me if I shouted they could hear it, although it would seem to them as though a boulder was talking to them. I did not bother asking what they'd do if that happened. I silently assumed it wouldn't be good or fun for us.

We watched for a while. Soon a helicopter landed outside the encirclement and eight well-suited men disembarked from its dark interior. They held various devices, some with lights, others looked like metal detectors or had vacuum sweepers and some had gadgets that didn't seem to do anything though I was sure they were taking readings of some kind or another. Once they had formed up they began a slow approach. I was relieved when nothing led them to the rock. I guessed Wind had done its best to take care of any give-away traces. Then one more man got out of the helicopter, very tall, suited, impassive, wearing black glasses, a real stinker. He stood, stared at the boulder and then got very busy on his cell phone while one of the others, clearly an assistant, used a satellite ready laptop and seemed feverishly busy. Meanwhile the armed men kept to the perimeter waiting on orders. My friend decided to go to sleep.

This was one slick trick; I was going to learn it for sure. I'd bet even Joey wouldn't know how it was done. I do not know when I fell asleep feeling safe as ever. I woke some time later and, using a mirror, I looked out to see. It had to be about noon; men were still around. A few were sitting right on top of us eating their lunches. It was eerie to see their butts squashed flat as they sat right on top of their quarry.

Now, in the daytime the shelter looked as if we were inside a fixed bubble of thick fog. I could hear the men sitting atop us easily and we listened on.

"Well, where to go from here, that's what I'd like to know."

"Damnedest thing I ever saw; there aren't any trails."

"Well," said a third man, "they've done that before. Their camp was right around here, not far from this rock yet there's nothing with a capital "N.""

"Well they've gone that's one thing sure."

"Correction, it is more accurate to say we have not been able to find them – here."

"What's the difference?"

"Well, truthfully speaking we can't prove they've left."

"Ok Mr. Smart Alec, what do you say to the fact that we know they are nowhere around for 40 miles or so. "

"Maybe they stood up on this here rock, jumped and flew away?" They all laughed heartily.

At the sound of the rude laughter, the real stinker, standing not far off, looked up, scowled their way and, dissatisfied, barked an order. I did not catch it though; they sure did. They buttoned up quick and went off in a group to meet two helicopters as they hove into view. They helped unload it and talked with the new men as they disembarked. As those copters took off another came into sight, circled the area, hovered for a moment over our "rock", and left.

The noise woke my friend. I asked, "We wait?"

"Yes, we wait."

"We cannot stay here for long, even if we are disguised."

"Why? We have fooled them."

"Maybe, for now. They followed us on foot. They know we did not go away on foot. They have an eye in the sky as you call it." I sensed his nodding. "Well, the rangers must have had satellite maps with detailed photos of this place before we got here and now, after, see? I don't think it'll take them long to get the idea that this rock has something to do with our disappearance – they'll try something, certainly.

"I understand; we must move – prepare yourself."

"Now? Don't we get out of here first, out of this thing we're in?"

"No, it will take us away."

"Are we going to the place-of-waiting?"

I was not looking at him when I said it. I could feel him wondering how I knew. "You said it in your sleep." Actually, I had heard him say it in a dream of mine.

He took it in stride, "That's where we go now."

He ignited a small bundle of incense, crusted with what I figured to be salt. I suddenly felt light-headed, sleepy and I laid back to rest even though I had the creepin' willy-nillies and seemed to be weightless.

Some Time or other - - -

Dear Joey,

I slept off and on – at least I think I did. I very much wanted to ask him something. Somehow or other I could not form complete thoughts. It seemed like days were passing by as I dozed. The weightlessness came and went, as did other sensations of movement. At times, it was as if we were adrift on a river of some kind. All the while, every time I looked he was keeping his face strictly intent upon the light from the candle he held to the edge of our enclosure. Although I couldn't see a thing, he peered out, as if he expected to see something important at any moment.

We eventually came to a steady rest and he began a song, which I loosely translate here:

> **Oh Heart of my Heart**
> **awaken, ye**
> **and spread your wings**
> **with such wishes as feather the air**
> **may this stone, protecting,**
> **hold safe the lives it bears**
> **help us hold fast to the truth**
> **let us be gone**
> **gone from the world**

**to travel with mountain, forest, stream and cloud
alive
from age to age
and transform as does soil to eye
of both deer and eagle
hearing what all-and-nothing tells
where
the breath of life
spills from every pore
where no tongue confuses the heart
where our soul will knit brilliant dreams
allowing us
to hail the soul,
enjoy the breath of life
and keep us seeking
Your Light
our eyes no longer seized by the illusions:
we give all, we do not have life
our lives are your life**

"We are here," he said as I awoke again. "Are you ready?"

"Do I've a choice?"

"No, not really, nor do I."

"Okay."

He sat there, after a moment of quiet; he took in a deep breath. Hw blew out a segment of the salt in the line he'd had made. The darkness began to lighten into grey. In a matter of moments, the fog about us dissolved as mist would in a slight breeze.

We were still inside the line he had drawn, with our pile of gear upon the same hard sandy ground we'd been on but all around that was a new fresh and verdant world. Cautiously, I stood up.

There was a flat grassy plain extending for as far as the eye could see. There were no distant mountain ranges either – only some rolling hills far to what I figured to be the east. He looked at me, made a sweeping gesture toward it, and cast his glance to indicate the four directions before he touched at his heart. He offered me some salt – all this was now my "inheritance" from his people; the place-of-waiting was for me too. I took him at his unspoken word – took his hand, on that. I could do no less after our escape escapade. We embraced each other as family and I became a child of his by virtue of our silent oaths.

There were thousands of boulders strewn about far and wide. He says each carries occupants as mysteriously as we had been. I asked if this was the past, present, or future; he said he wasn't sure. I was shaken. He brought me to my by asking if I thought the men looking for us could get here; I immediately knew they couldn't. I don't know what those folks saw when we left. I guess it doesn't matter – to us anyway. What's done is done. I intend to find out about the time aspect, if it's possible. The Wind's here though it gives little aid. In fact, it comes around only rarely though it has become quite annoyingly good at checkers and highly sarcastic.

************************ **********************

The Appendixes

************************ **********************

A Call For Help!

I looked over my copy of what I wrote way back when, partly to prepare for going back. The old man will not be with me so I'm leaving this note to append my old diary even though I didn't write a thing since I reworked it all those years ago when I sent it back. I noticed lots of errors and inconsistencies although I cannot recall much – I decided to leave well enough alone.

At first, I was learning so much, we were busy all the time, for years, while nothing much happened; I mean to say it has only been he, Wind, nature, and I.

Well, I've grown a great deal while my friend looks a lot younger than he aught to. For him, being here, changes his aging process, so he says. Then again, there's no one here to compare him with. It's gotten so we don't even have much to say, besides talking about food, fishing, the weather, or new uses for plants or making better recipes. We sound like a pair of elders on permanent leave of our responsibilities, except we don't complain about aches and pains, our bowels, their movements, or a lack thereof, nor peeing, its color, or conditions. I haven't grown a lick in a long run of seasons, which means I'm probably an adult.

We have some rockwork structures, a granary, and a couple of workhouses with storage vaults built into the hillside, which we fixed up using a natural cave for a start. Our garden is nice. It's quite stable and in its tenth season. Oh, we do go on walk-abouts together or, sometimes, by ourselves mainly to keep sharp. Why it was only a few days ago when I laughed, after he said he thought I was getting fat – as if he should talk.

And wouldn't you know I'm up and having to leave just after we got all settled comfy-cozy in a permanent camp. In a way, we've had a long, long vacation but now it is over. Here is what happened.

A couple of days back, Wind began kicking up dust and quickly worked up into a howling. It was such a sudden, righteous squall, we barely had time to eye each other some serious questions before it fell wildly upon our camp. The air cut in sharp, whistled all around, and drenched us as it blew ice cold off and on. We had to crawl, fearing for our lives, toward the cave opening. Once inside without speaking we came to understand and wept uncontrollably over the cause of the trouble. Wind was crying or raging. It was insane with pain – somehow it was suffering mightily.

By the time we changed into some warm clothes, the storm had vanished. We stepped outside; I was glad the camp hadn't been harmed; all the hard buildings had stayed and the only noticeable loss was the checker set we'd made using carved shells for the pieces and obsidian along with stained schist for the board.

Again, as I sat down on a rock face whispering to Wind, heavy clouds boiled up on the near horizon and began racing toward us. The darkening front rushed closer as thunder roared and lightning flashed beneath it. We took a moment to study this burgeoning gloomy tumult as it approached. Soon a mass of fulminating chaos, of roiling clouds towered above us. The sky seemed to be rending itself. Again, Wind whipped up about our feet, lashed at us with sleet, pelted us with rock hard hail, and dust swirled in the mix nearly blinding us to boot. We were quicker about getting inside this time and we locked down before retreating to the back of the cave as the full violence hit our camp. This time it lasted for hours.

I couldn't stand it! I became sickened with headaches and body pains, had fits off and on, and vomited. I began to have trouble breathing as we angrily waited it out. When I could not take it, I bolted for the outside, he got a grip on me but I slipped my coat and got away. I foolishly made it outside, stood my ground and screamed repeatedly for help until a branch flew out of the chaos, hit me, and it was lights out. I came to as he was tending me. I could see he'd been bruised about his face, presumably when he went out to drag me back in. My head hurt; I was aching all over as if I'd been beaten; I had been. He told me the sky had cleared.

When I winced as I tried to get up he said, "You got a brain that needs some serious back fill."

"You got a lump on that thing you call a head."

"Thanks for reminding me. Are you ok, I mean, for real?"

"Yes, really," I said, although I wasn't sure.

"Wind told me you have to go back; you have to help."

I wasn't surprised Wind had spoken to him. What surprised was my reaction – simple acceptance.

"Yes, I know. Will you show me how to prepare salt?"

"It's been ready for years, just for you and I've already set it out." He nodded, indicating a nearly closed white circle in the dust not a few yards from the opening of our cave.

"What do I need to know?"

"Keep the salt you will use for your return on you at all times; you never know, also you need only the thinnest line yet it must be in soil and solid. It will work as soon as you know it will. Also, you'll be on your own. You will travel wherever water flows. Time means nothing. Avoid getting hung up on dry land because then you'll have to wait for an ocean. As pilot, it will seem as though you are in a clear bubble. You'll use a light to keep focused, though it is your insight, intuition or dreams that will guide you as much as your memory might but keep in mind the needs of your journey that will be your compass. After this voyage, nothing will be a blank to you, which is both the good news and the bad, in terms of what you'll take away. I am sorry you'll have to go through that."

I wondered what he meant. It was time to go. All I knew was I didn't know what to expect.

"Oh by the way, don't you want my real name before you go?"

"What?"

"I thought you could hear like a bat."

"All this time goes by and you decide now to tell me now?"

"That's right, I think you should know."

"Why now?"

"No time like the present."

I appreciated the dry witticism, "Well, what is it?"

"You can call me Mr. Fish."

"Mr. Fish?"

"Do you have a hearing problem?"

"No" He stood there waiting.

"Mr. Fish?"

"It's a joke; don't bother laughing; you'll get it later, what about your name?"

"You mean besides Windfoot?"

"Yes."

"You can call me Jan."

We looked at each other, shrugged and I that was the last I thought I'd see of him.

********************* *********************

My Return

My first notes:

I arrived in the east bay hills of the San Francisco Bay Area. I could see a valley in the distance filled with suburbanized land cover. I know now what he meant about memory being a guide with time travel. From the perspective of a pilot, I can say it looked as though I was sailing over a fluid landscape as seasonal lights flickered. I could follow water currents as they flowed over the land, which changed shape during time. It was a wild ride and, as he'd said, it was memory, which guided me back to a place where my intuition clicked. I decided to hold up by blowing out the candle I used and then, waiting until daylight, I dissolved the shape. I got still, called to Wind. In a moment, it brought me food before lifting me over to a place a quarter mile beyond some housing.

I walked downhill into town and found a library. Computers are amazing things and Joey, or what seems like Joey, took to them instantly. We learned how science, using what they knew of my ability, had spawned a tremendously powerful technology. In secret, using something called HYDRA, a cabal of men had begun directing weather and or its conditions to affect a country or regional politics – meaning who was allowed to live or die – all over the world. It was new, effective, and hidden well enough – for although there was no accurate description of the project in public policy, there were budget items, the direction of certain research grants, and a list of ongoing projects in evidence. Individually they meant little, but I quickly learned what to look for and put the puzzle together. Amazingly, no one, not even America's enemies, knew what was going on. Joey, we, I mean I, could hack, and understood how disparate projects weren't seen in terms of how they had been combined to manifest the primary effect – which was devastating – even horrifically so. We figured HYDRA was the cause of Wind's problem though we couldn't determine who was behind it or where it was.

I went outside, sat still for Wind. After asking, I was told it was being forced to deliver effects, driven by maddening, blinding pain. Once the heat, which always comes from above, starts, it gets very tired no matter how it fights then it "forgets" itself – at least for a while. It is only some days afterwards, when memories bubble up, that the truth is revealed. Wind was remorseful; things died and even the earth is sad when the pain drives wind to do this evil work. What frightened Wind was it felt very ill for a long time after each abuse and it was always getting harder to resist. I understood, when under such pain, Wind would not be available to me.

"It is as if, during the crime, I am not in this time. I cry elsewhere or when and it is why I had to find you way far away there through the me that is up in that when and that where"

"You could have spoken more clearly; by the way."

Wind was silent.

I wanted another run at the computer; to find names or concrete details however as I stood to go back inside, sirens started up. They were not far off and converging fast. It was worse than in old days; they were much quicker about detecting me. Since I was in the open near down town, I sprinted away as if to catch a bus, which was just pulling into a stop down the block. A man even tried to get the bus to stop for me, he failed, and I slowed then came to a panting halt. I went around the corner as if to go along the route but took off in an easy lope. I followed the wind, which led me, though oddly, until I fell in with a group of casual joggers. Police cars were still closing on the area around the library but by then I was several blocks away. When a police unit went past my group of joggers, going the wrong way, and fast, I allowed my self a brief sense of relief. I slowly dropped to the back of the pack. None of them noticed as I jogged off onto a golf course, heading for the hills. I got into the trees before I stopped to catch my breath and think for a moment.

I heard sirens on three sides of my position although they were not converging. Joey's voice said the science of this time allowed them to track me not only by the imprint I leave on atmospheric patterns – whenever Wind is in contact with me – but by my EMT signal as well. Joey said the EMT activity of a human brain could be detected and signal location can be fed to a satellite. Since mine was very much stronger and was an associated phenomenon with that of Wind – they'd found a way to read or detect me, even if indirectly, it seemed. I wondered; if they could track when I was using my intuition or dreaming. Joey said he didn't know.

I kept my thoughts small as I huffed hard uphill. I heard helicopters approach the area but their search pattern was taking them away from me. I kept on. For a couple of hours I was striding along. For a moment, the treetops around me got into a familiar motioning. I guessed Wind was either having fun with my pursuers or trying to find me.

Wind guided me uphill only to rush around behind me. A moment later, in a snap, Wind was gone. I began to hear approaching dirt bikes as well as some voices. I continued uphill keeping to cover and under trees. I seriously mulled pulling out the salt and was looking for spots as I ran. Again, Wind came back, acted up behind me both to the left and right – then it was gone.

I found a two-lane road and began a well paced jog until a got a lift from a man hauling junk. We talked for a while, especially about the police vehicles, which passed us going pell-mell the other way. I got out when he turned off to head toward the bay. I had gone at least 40 miles; if I watched myself, I could keep a low profile. I wouldn't call on Wind, yet.

The long distance runs I had taken in the other world helped here. I got another ride too so I was thinking I had made a get away by the time I hopped off.

Yet, hours later I was sprinting over the parking grounds for Mount Diablo's newly remade Overlook Center built onto and into the eastern face of its rocky slope. I had lost Wind somehow and my pursuers had forced me toward the place. I'd been shot at a couple of times so I had no plan B as I headed for the building itself. Behind me, Wind came up and swept the area clear of those pursuing me on foot and their dogs. Once I got inside the weather change was immediate and intense. All around a terrific lightning storm broke; torrents of rain poured. Everyone inside was amazed at the incredibly violent display of electrical force. When, just as suddenly, it lost energy, dissipated, and the sun came out.

From one of the stained glass windows on the upper floor of the facility I watched a storm rage back only to be swept away. In the brief interval, six large military helicopters flew in and hovered as they dropped off a dozens of men. They began firing at the building as they took up positions surrounding it. They shot anything that moved. The many tourists, those who'd taken shelter from the storm, as well as those in the shops or who were dining got down on the floor quickly although a number were killed outright in the first fusillade. The survivors were scared to death by the incessant sniping. Some tried to bring wounded into safety; a couple of them died for their trouble. Wind came and went at rapid intervals. Inside, the TV in the bar was on. I could hear the media reporting a terrorist attack at the Overlook. It said the military was getting demands over the phone even as hostages were being executed. It said the police forces; rangers and military Special Forces surrounding the place were taking heavy casualties. In addition, the broadcast signals from the scene cut out as the bizarre weather complicated matters somehow.

While we had some cover, due to the storm, people began to organize. Thanks to Joey's memorizing of emergency manuals, I was a real help to the doctor and two ER nurses that happened to be there. We saved at least a couple of lives, treated some others as we got everyone into safe positions. The storm let up for a moment though not completely and sniping started up again.

I was finishing a splint on boy when they began talking at us with a megaphone. They addressed the "terrorists." They were willing to continue talking by phone but wanted to talk with one in particular. By describing me, and what I was wearing, the people inside knew I was the one they wanted. Some of them flew off their respective handles, whipped themselves into an uproar, and a wild bunch rushed me. Fortunately and unfortunately, a few of those were shot from the outside as they rushed me and the others ducked back down. Many seemed confused by the facts. First, there was no group of terrorists. Second, I had been helping them. Third, anyone that tried to signal outside was shot at and, last, I hadn't any weapons so I couldn't be responsible for any of the deaths – yet the TV was saying I was "with the terrorists" and most of them looked at me with a mixture disbelief, dismay and anger.

I was amazed at how evident truth did not matter to some of them probably because they were trapped, in immanent danger, and could not think straight to save their lives, literally. I tried to explain only to be shouted down. Doctor Marslow, with blood still on his hands, hollered at them all, finally deriding them into an embarrassed silence. I'd saved lives he said, gesturing to the four grateful families. In an eerie silence he tried to get them to understand, to remember, since everyone's cell phone was out and the building's phones lines were dead – it was impossible for anyone in here make any demands by phone to anyone and certainly no one had seen me on any kind of phone. Amazingly, this went nowhere with some who insisted they'd be safe if I'd just give myself up. These could not be swayed from their point of view, which after all, had a grain of truth to it.

A vet, Thomas Gerard, had taken the liberty of securing the few weapons he could find, shot a few rounds into the air, punctuating his calls for them to, "Shut up, shut up, shut up!" he yelled. "All this man wants to do is escape. I'm military and I'm tellin' ya, that ain't no military operation; no sir, no government troops would fire indiscriminately on US citizens like this. Lastly, I got the only guns in here; so you can all just settle down real nice like, quickly and quietly!" He had their attention by gumbo. He finished, flourishing his two hand guns, "Oh, yeah, if any of you want to leave, be my guest. Certainly. You are perfectly free to do so; I won't get in your way. See if you can get out of here without being shot for your kind trouble." There was profound silence amongst us all, which we could discern despite the windstorm outside and constant patter of bullets hitting all around inside the building.

I appreciated his efforts. It was clear lies were being spread everywhere outside. His truth did not matter nor did anyone's beliefs about me. I was certain, at some point, those outside would attack using even more violence and was thinking that the fact they hadn't done so was proof I was wanted alive.

Gerard, Marslow, a few others, and I hunkered down. I have to say Gerard sounded much like a certain, Mr. Fish, as he quietly argued some others into siding with me. He was an organizer too. Soon we had teams set up to care for wounded, move people to the basement and to secure food and water. We wracked our brains figure a safe way, some kind of trick or other, which would get at least some of them out alive if circumstances allowed. Then too, whenever Wind died down, I fired off a few rounds from different locations using different guns to keep them guessing; a fusillade from without always ensued; they had at least one heavy machine gun. Then, there was a sudden cessation.

Moments later I heard a phone ringing and a voice from the megaphone outside advised me it was my mother calling and that she was at the scene. They wanted to her talk with me in person. I was suspicious but felt oddly confident, even happy.

************************ ************************

Marie's Epilogue

Thank you for sending on your diary; I read it in one sitting the day I was allowed to see it. I was surprised, at first, when they gave it to me. However, I have to say, as a mother, I am gratified deeply. So much has happened since you left and so much more in the brief time you've been back. The world is still crazy, but some say there is change in the air. When I talk to ordinary people, not my handlers or personal assistants, as they call themselves, I hear many say they believe things are going to get very much better and very soon. Of course, I know now you sent the book to me years ago and I was only allowed to see it much later in the hopes that I'd proceed to give some secret away. I don't know that I did. Back then, well, it was a different world. Now, I guess, that those who hoped to use it to find you, in order to use you as they do that awful machine in the arctic, maybe didn't read it so well themselves.

I've written this to you, for the record.

Let me catch you up. Of course, your disappearance was horrible for me. I blamed Vince. After we reported you missing Vince got worried he'd somehow loose jobs, friends or have all sorts of problems because of you and what you did. I suspected he deeply feared getting into an emotional entanglement he could not understand or deal with. He did surprise me though, I've to say, when he expressed real concern for you then pride when you made your own way, showing some "real balls" – you know Vince.

Anyway, it was ordinary at first, by which I meant during the first few days it was hard to get through to anyone in charge of your case and when we finally did we could tell nothing was being done. Vince and I argued all over that believe you me but over time we both changed, and how!

Some few months on, early one Sunday morning, after playing cards with some friends and drinking but, and I have to add here, we only got a little lightheaded. We giggled it up after dinner, talked until late, but were fast asleep before midnight. Well, approaching sirens woke us both up. Vince went to the bathroom while I tried to go back to sleep. Both of us thought it had to do with a spate of rough burglaries in our neighborhood so we were glad for the attention. After the sirens stopped near by, both us cuddled and hoped to snooze through whatever it was.

Then there came a hammering at our front door. I was alarmed because of the violence of it. Vince went to look but when the door began splintering and breaking of its hinges. Vince snapped. He came back and took the 44's he kept in the room, always loaded, stood and began firing toward front door. I threw open a window, tossed out some blankets, and dove under the bed. Vince ducked and rolled to fire again. I heard lots of gunfire and then it all went quiet.

I could see Vince on the floor. The police entered the room and two of them took him up but he seemed limp, I was sure he was faking it. It took them so long to find me I thought I was going make it out of there. I found out later Vince had been knocked out by a rubber bullet. Luckily, no one was killed but Vince wounded nine officers, a couple badly.

They took us into custody. From then on we were confused as to why they were holding us, what the charges were, who or what agency or agencies were involved as well as, who had control of the case, why it was such a big deal or how you and we were involved in different ways according to different people. We, both of us, came to believe, independently mind, that we were being lied to from the get go, although we both had our own reasons for believing that. Of course, lawyers only made things worse. There were different lawyers saying different things to everyone, the press, us as well as each other. We stood accused of everything from child abuse to terrorism. The whole thing kept getting bigger. You were in the news a good deal for a while as was anyone that ever knew us, assholes included. We were photographed each time we went in or out of any building; it was a blizzard of chaos; fame has its price.

Finally, there was a hearing, behind closed doors. We did not want to go to jail for umpteen years, so we agreed to do as they asked. We were put under house arrest and have people assigned to us, observers in our neighborhood, in our building and, off and on, these so-called friends from out of town would stay with us. We agreed to a mandatory health regimen, counseling and to be available at any time should they have need to talk to us or have us talk with you, Jan, should it ever become possible.

We did as told for years on end. Eventually things died down. We were glad to be out of the news living "ordinary lives" in something like a witness protection program. We still assumed they were lying to us, one way or another. Vince pegged it when he said, "a smaller truth in the service of a broader lie is a lie for all that."

For years we knew only what they told us although we never had any idea what the truth was. For our part, we both told the truth to keep things simple, if only for us. Where we disagreed, and they caught us out a few times, we argued in front of them. Our one aim was to have them think we were helping as best we could. Between us, however, we tried to throw monkey wrenches into the works whenever possible. It was not hard to plant a falsie since we knew we were bugged six ways to Sunday. No matter where we were or what we were doing, we were never truly alone. We tested them all sorts of ways when we were alone by writing notes, whispering, making drawings or tapping signals; each time the phone would ring, a car would go by, a neighbor stop in, someone would walk around a corner or we'd be "invited" to spend time with our "friends." We became a campaign issue for goodness sakes. Conservatives talked about, guess what, family values while the so-called liberals went on about funding for childcare and family services. We had interviews; it was interminable.

They said you were in-cahoots with some violent, crazy people, an American Indian for one, who they said was a known terrorist responsible for some of the mayhem the press attributed to you. He was at your side in aerial and long distance photos. We heard tapes of a man, said to be him, making threats. They said they were using satellites in the hunt as well as a wide-ranging network of volunteers.

Then, after years of finagling, we finally talked them into letting us take a long day hike; we couldn't get them to let us camp. It was a nice enough day until someone began shooting at us killing one of the guards and wounding the others. Vince and I got a hold of the guns and took out a few of the shooters as they broke cover firing as they advanced. We ran out of ammo and ran. They chased after us taking shots as they did so. Very quickly even more people showed up and there was a firefight. In the chaos each of us tried to escape. Vince was wounded several times after he tried to shoot his way out. I hijacked a police car but I couldn't get to a place where I could ditch it. After I mistakenly got on to a freeway they shot out the tires and I lost control. I was injured considerably as were others, in the ensuing pile up.

Later, they showed us letters they'd received providing support for their belief that we were under threat from various crazies for one reason or another. Of course, we both dismissed such things quietly.

It seemed like a miracle but we fell in love again and it was beautiful, for a time. However, after a several years, we gradually fell out and this time it seemed quite natural. After we separated, we saw each other only during our appointments where, often enough, they apprised us of what you were doing as best they were able. They always asked if you'd been in contact as if that was possible without them knowing or if it had happened that we'd tell them. We believed your trail had gone cold. My guess was they held onto us in the hopes of getting to you.

Over the years they told us you were a drug mule, an arsonist, a burglar traveling with a gang of thugs responsible for a number of deaths not to mention the disablement of dozens more – even gun running and murdering. We couldn't believe it; I couldn't, in my heart. Vince spoke up to the people we dealt with even though he knew nothing he could say would alter their perceptions of you, him or me. It was good to see the nice, brave, honest side of him. As the years went by, we could only wonder if they would ever let us go.

Therefore, when the news began reporting that terrorists had taken hostages at the Overlook, it was not unusual for me to take an interest in someone else's problems. There were many reported casualties as a full military presence was trying to retake the building. Like I say, we had been separated so I don't know what that day was like for Vince. I watched events unfold. The TV showed soldiers being treated in the field. There were many dead, civilians too. It was awful.

Of course, I didn't, even then, know you were there. I was scared for the poor people inside, especially after the army had some armored vehicles on the way. What kept me glued to the set was the crazy storm holding over the mountain. The weather reporter kept saying it was 'radically bizarre." The military and police said it was making their operations nearly impossible and causing a number of the casualties. From time to time, hurricane force winds cleared vehicles off parking lots or from the road leading up to the place. There were, for a time, a couple of dark whirling funnel clouds, twisters. One held a position on the main roadway up while the other meandered, dipping down every now and then to overturn armored cars, tanks or other vehicles. There was lots of lightning. The severe rainfall caused flooding along with widespread power outages in all the nearby towns. The government was telling people to evacuate; it was crazy squared and the world was following the story.

They kept saying there was only one photo of one terrorist, which they showed repeatedly but since it was taken through a tinted window all I could see was a tall, slender person in sepia tones. Also, the image was half in and half out of the dark. This, we were told, was the mastermind.

When a computer enhancement of the image was modeled; my heart skipped a beat or two. I knew it was you. I almost said something although I had the presence of mind to stifle it. I did not want my roommate to understand what I had come to know. Since Vince had gone, I'd taken up my own strategies and, being free to fight in my own way, had been serving up disinformation wherever I could. I had been telling them about dreams with you while making up some "long lost memories" in therapy. As far as I could tell they'd been buying my guff hook, line, and sinker – though I did not know to what extent it was helpful.

When my "roomie" walked in; I blurted out what was happening. She was not interested. I stayed glued to the tube watching the news, as would anyone normal I guess.

While it wasn't unusual to hear the sound of keys in the lock or the clumping shoes of unknown men approach, still I was surprised and had the presence of mind to toughen up to prepare. I enjoyed being a few steps ahead of them. There were four men with a woman in command. Two men hoisted me out of my chair, another gave me my coat, and I was hustled into a limousine, which took me to a waiting helicopter in a nearby park. No one said a word. Although I knew where we were going, I acted surprised when they told me about you. I became purposefully subdued thereafter. In fact, I said nothing. This frustrated the woman in charge to no end. I laughed, inside of course, while playing my hand to the hilt. She was flushed; I was radiant, again, inside. I did it so well because, truly, although I could not care less, I didn't have to give anything away. No matter what she said, I looked away, closed my eyes without responding. When she slapped me; I busted a good sharp backhand slashing a deep cut in her pert pretty little face with my handcuffs.

Turbulence shook the helicopter like nothing else I'd ever felt, the lights flickered; we lost altitude drastically. I got a few good kicks in on "Madam Butterfly" knocking her out. No one noticed in the chaos leading up to a very hard landing. After we got out, I saw Vince had been brought too. We could only look at each other from a distance. They took me directly up to the scene. They wanted to me to talk to you. There was no debating with these people; they believed the lies they were repeating. I knew you were not with a bunch of terrorists. I suspected they'd been doing all the shooting thus all the killing and that there were no terrorists inside, nor hostages. It was insane. They said you had asked to speak with me a number of times, which made me happy but I now know it was just another lie.

Now, although I don't recall most of what we said back then but I can tell you almost all of what I said was scripted. I had an implant some years back; they could listen in on anything I said as well as tell me what to say. I hoped you had enough doubts about everything to expect something like that. If I had refused, their back up was to have someone imitating my voice over a PA to try to get what they wanted, if they could. I assumed Vince had absolutely refused to cooperate, good for him. They were ready for any contingency, the whole nine yards. I did not have to be told that, if I or we failed, we'd both have some real hard times again as would our relatives, again, the whole nine yards. Your life was at stake too – even though they said they wanted you alive and well.

The storm would come in a rage and clear off as if it was caught in a wavering struggle. They brought me to the top during a lull. I was instructed to walk across the plaza. I had no choice in any of this not what I'd say, do or have to try when the time came. When you beckoned me inside I was told to follow your lead.

I hardly knew you, but your face was right as rain. I cried; I apologize for the life you had all those years ago. I was glad, though, when you spoke kindly to me. I had no reason to expect you to forgive me, thank you for that.

I told you what they told me to say even as we wrote notes back and forth or signaled. Thank you for your loving expressions. We had such little time. You had been calling Wind with no result. We worried if the weather cleared or the military men got confident, they'd rush the place. I scribbled I'd heard one of them say they were getting better at distracting Wind. As instructed I made the threats and promises to you until everyone in the place was clear about what the consequences to me were unless you got into a containment van. Although I am sorry I went along with them, it was the only way to get to you. The only way I could try to help or make up for what I did to you. I hope these notes make that clear. I knew we were still family still, even then, after such great distances of time and space.

I can still see the vehicle arriving, a custom built thing that looked like an armored semi-trailer built onto a pair of tank chassis.

I was very proud of you when you stood up to everyone saying you could deal with them from anywhere. When you began to walk toward a torn opening in the building, I will always thank that man; the one so friendly to us both, who stood up, blocked your way, and insisted you not go alone. You'd saved his wife's life. I remember the handful of volunteers clamoring to form a human shield and how you stood listening to them before dismissing their offers and commanded them to leave off. You did not want them in danger. However, it took, Tom, the fiery vet, to get them all to stand down. I knew you were going to go inside the beast to sacrifice yourself – hoping to use its violence, one way or another, to destroy it. I couldn't have been prouder when you said, "Mom, I just want no more blood on our hands."

************************ **********************

Excerpts from An Old Man's View

It was not the sound of the wind, which caused everyone watching you walk toward the truck to look up. They had to wonder why the sky darkened so rapidly or why the dark clouds were moving without a breath of wind. They did not comprehend the reality behind the sound that many billions of insects made before those myriads fell upon the scene creating instant blinding chaos. Then these were joined by multitudes of animals, reptiles, dogs, cats – everything from squirrels to bears, hummingbirds to eagles got all over every soldier or military vehicle surrounding the building.

Up in the peaceful lands I had told the ancestors Wind was dying. It had come back in pain. I believed, at that time, you had failed. The ancestors agreed, so I was allowed to return. They also granted me some songs and, in dreams, taught me "to go a'calling." All the little beings answered with much rage in their hearts; all were very willing, no eager; to deliver a message to human kind – such as was long overdue.

Of course, the humans would not give up. I knew this too. I heard the suffering sounds of anguish as I rode up the slope of Mount Diablo on a good pony, a truly great being – one that only wanted to help. He saved me twice and for all his effort he was murdered. It was the saddest moment in my life, seeing his eyes call to mine as their light faded away.

I do not know how I got to the building or, for that matter, got inside alive. I believed I had brought help though even as I sat with you and your mother the battle outside was quieting. The army used a device, which confused the insects; and they began to disperse. Soon the battle was only against the larger animals and humans had a great advantage with their guns and other bizarre weapons. Just as we wondered if it was over a storm came back howling from the north clearing the air of insects but it wasn't your Wind, Jan. The men outside began a murderous fusillade targeting everything that moved as they began a determined advance.

We were confused. No one had any idea what was going on. The group of us huddling with you took up arms. We began shooting blindly from cover if only to slow them down. Your mom wondered, out loud, if the birds had been harmed when the

Wind was forcefully directed as this one was. That's when you sat back, stunned, an idea, its proper time arrived, had dawned. You talked to the flying ones through your ring.

They knew where the machine, used to hurt the wind, was. They too had suffered each time it had been used – however they had not connected the cause with its other global effects. You and they put the puzzle together then helped each other see way up into the far northern part of the world where, in a vast frozen waste, the buildings housing the monstrous device sat peaceably unmolested. So we, your mother, I, and a couple of the others with us, did as you asked. We sat in a circle, held hands and together helped you call into the far north of the world. I went a calling through you and with the ring. We told the winged ones and the other beings what had to be done. Soon birds fell upon the place. Any human they happened across was harassed run off. They took down planes. Polar bear brothers and sisters broke through the simple fencing, tore apart flimsy buildings and destroyed the fragile, sensitive array of antennae. Many people were chased off into the murderously cold waste surrounding the base where they perished. The place was soon a burning wreck. Though we rejoiced where we sat in circle, Wind still would not answer. We huddled in fear.

Outside the fight raged if anything more loudly than ever before – even more animals came and threw themselves into the blazing weapon's fire used by the humans. We all prayed and you, Jan, prayed for Wind by whistling for it.

You were in a deeply trance-like state mumbling. This continued despite the chaotic cacophony of rage tearing all about the outside. The animals were not giving up. We, inside, could hear the sound of the struggle growing both louder and closer. The killing was great; the din of battle deafening as voices of men were heard not far off; all the while bullets zinged, zipped, or ricocheted near to where we hid.

Wind did come. We felt it. Then, and quite soon, we heard the oddest piping whistling sounds all around us as the gunfire ceased. We heard cries of both man and beast. In a matter of minutes, all the noise faded and it was absolutely still. Wind had unwound. For long seeming minutes, we listened to the silence.

We stayed crouched in hiding until a redwing black bird swooped in through the gaping hole in the wall, flitted over to us to gently land on the back of a nearby chair. He looked us over; curiously, chirped once then darted quickly back outside where it started singing to beat the band. That's when we stood up, except you remained in a trance. We all looked down at you. No one wanted to touch or disturb you in any way. A fox came and a brown bear with a bad limp came in to that same gaping hole. They stood outside, looking us over. When a coyote called, they both turned to look in that direction. They turned to look at us again though only for a moment, before ambling off. We slowly walked outside. The bear reclined a few yards off, apparently, waiting for us. After we came out, he got up, walked over, sniffed us one by one and lay back down to doze.

Dead were heaped all around. There were many, many animals, big and small, many soldiers too. There was an odd thing about all those soldiers; none of them had weapons anywhere near them. Most had some or all of their clothes torn up or off. All other gear was scattered widely.

We did not know what had happened. I knew you did. I went back inside only to find you had collapsed into a deep sleep. I checked all your pulses; they were fine. When I looked up, I saw the bear and a wolf had joined me. Together we stood watch; your mom did not leave your side, even when she slept.

When your eyes opened, it was only for a moment to meet mine. You told me Wind had learned its torture was only partly due to the machine. Much of its extreme suffering was due to the fact it had been driven to kill for a long, long time, without knowing. It now believed killing was a result of civilization, at least as it had been known. Then you seemed deeply tired, nodded out only to come to and ask if you were safe. I reassured you. Then you fell into a deep slumber, though I wondered if you really slept.

Every once in a while, I'd swear, I heard you whisper as a number of the animals, which had taken up roles of support around you, would look as a one directly at you. Always, some few would go off directly while others would settle in to replace them. As I say, I did not think you were just lying there.

I watched the sunrise the next day from the roof of the building. From its highest peak, I watched the beginning of first day of what became a new world.

During the first few days, anyone who could walk left. The emergency vehicles could not get within half a mile of the place because of the damage to the roadway, blockage by ruined vehicles and the mounds of dead. A medical team had blazed a trail through it all. They let us know there was a station being put together down the road where they'd treat anyone who needed it. Law enforcement officers promised to get every one home. Your mom pitched in down there driving trucks and organizing convoys to get folks home and transport supplies. She did not come back, which was sad. She still had to deal with them even if in her own way; she'd indicated as much. She is a brave and fine woman. I will miss her.

All the while, you lay there; we set up watch and stayed on. There was plenty of food since the animals kept bringing us fruit and all sorts of goodies from stores; it was a sweet set up in that regard.

When you came to, after three days, the many bodies had been taken off; the place had been quite cleared up. You said you did not know what to do besides stay on here so we did. I had nothing better to do; I told you that. We set up camp in the building. You would go for walks with the various animals as birds came and went from your shoulder often. We had some very good checker games, told stories and sang – just like the old times way "up there."

You did tell me about Wind during the time we shared. These things are what I recalled. You said it all began long ago with the practical use of fire and the landscape changes humans manifested due to its use and their invention of agriculture. Such things were perceptible to Wind. For a time, Wind played with these things and so helped people unwittingly. It appreciated the burning of incense or other sensory plumes, music, dance and especially singing, which was what had it come to see it was an animal that was source of all of those other phenomena.

It became aware of humans through their songs, music and dance because such things were able to affect its body; and this, in turn, led it to become self-aware. You said it liked such effects so much it came to believe it was being called so that, over time, it came to be just that way. It brought rains to thirsting lands or cleared clouds allowing warmth and light to reach places of singing and music. You once said Wind liked the patterns music created in it; it said music was the only beautiful sound humans made. When you told me, I believed you: it explained some mystery stories of my peoples.

Through the ages, Wind acted variously to affect human history although it was blind, deaf and dumb as to the effects it was causing, even as it suffered, to some degree because of what it did.

You said Wind had not knowingly gotten involved with human affairs until human affairs began to threaten its life earlier, during the last century, mainly because of the very large scale wars not to mention the development of atomic bombs, which prompted it to understand humans were connected to its distress as their massive efforts to kill each other on an industrial scale caused Wind collateral damage. It learned to bring rain to battlefields purposely not incidentally as it had done before.

While it knew humanity was harmful, some time passed as it wondered what to do. When this problem became dire and urgent action was demanded for survival's sake, its evolution and development was driven toward an ever-higher consciousness. You said Wind had reconciled with God, who agreed that its existence and consciousness impelled it to engage with humans.

So there came a time when, in Winds own interest of survival, it had to intervene directly in human affairs. It sought out someone who wanted to hear what it had to say, one who could speak to it. That's how it found you, Jan, or how you, in your needs, found Wind; I put that together from what you were muttering and what the old family stories had said.

You told me on that horrific day you had commanded Wind to kill, not knowing it could not or would not do so. You told me it had said it could never again kill as it had before without knowing or at the behest of anyone. Killing hurt it, no matter who died. You said Wind could have died from its abuse and all life would be sorely put to the test until it was reborn again.

This explained why Wind had only disarmed the humans attacking the Overlook, whisking away their weapons – the piping sound we'd heard was Wind intoning as it moved through the rifling of gun barrels; it was this grip which allowed to hurl the guns far away. This is why it turned over tanks or forced aircraft down. It explained why it was the animals that finally put all the humans to flight. Wind knew animals and insects, being mortal, understood life and death; that they, therefore, could deal in it and still survive the experience. It sounded right to me; I know animals, to them, nothing ever goes to waste, every little being serves, even if only by decomposing.

Together Wind, the little beings, and you, using your ring, routed human armed forces the world over.

We were completely safe. We were left alone for months. However, one day, you turned to me, apropos of nothing, and said we no longer needed to stay. By that time, of course, it was just we two. On our way down the mountain, nothing seemed different. We could see farms, fields, highways and byways. After we got to first intersection, our animal friends left us with a graceful ceremony of their own creation. When we walked into town, no one took much notice. No one knew who we were and we were glad of that.

We went to a café to have brunch. The paper told me how much the world had changed in those few months. Wind had taken every nuclear device off the planet, hurling them into space. They were now falling into the sun. Conventional wars could no longer happen when weapons were ripped from the hands of soldiers or their great machines were tossed about as if toys. Navies could not sail with ill intent. The paper was still full of the many miracles, which happened during the vast struggle and later during the time Wind destroyed military installations around the world. Warfare was no more.

I told you I was going to continue on my way home and invited you to come sometime to see my people. You promised you would. You took the check and paid for it. Unexpectedly wordless, we stood outside for a while as if looking around for something. We simply shook hands and walked away from each other. I turned to look at you go; you did not do the same. I prayed. I was happy. I was going home. I could live happy now. My ancestors were smiling.

While I don't know what will come of this, it is a new age – truly and a great wonder. It feels good. You are the Wind's Wonder as it has told me. Yes, I hear it now too; there are a few who have been elected. I only hope that seven, seventy or seven hundred generations from now we'll all still feel this same way. With all due respect, George flows in Water ... AKA Fish.

Yes! Give this book away!

When you give this book away, please initial it here and indicate where and when you handed it off. I'd like these to meander the world over and perhaps migrate back to San Francisco someday as kind of message in a bottle. I look forward to its MUNI debut, finding it at a garage sale, or on a shelf in a used bookstore.

Initials	City	Date

Once this page is full, please use any other page – go for it!